Priceless Treasure

Book Four in The Lost Andersons

By
MELODY ANNE

PRICELESS TREASURE
Book Four in The Lost Andersons

Copyright © 2015 Melody Anne

Published by: Eternal Dreams

ISBN-13: 978-1517289188
ISBN-10: 1517289181

Cover Art by Edward
Edited by Alison
Interior Design by Adam

www.melodyanne.com

Email: info@melodyanne.com

 /MelodyAnneAuthor  @AuthMelodyAnne

First Edition
Printed in the USA

DEDICATION

This is dedicated to my niece Brianne who has grown up to be an incredibly kind, beautiful, amazing young woman. I love you with all my heart.

OTHER BOOKS BY MELODY ANNE

Billionaire Bachelors:
*The Billionaire Wins the Game
*The Billionaire's Dance
*The Billionaire Falls - Amazon
*The Billionaire's Marriage Proposal
*Blackmailing the Billionaire
*Run Away Heiress
*The Billionaire's Final Stand

The Lost Andersons:
*Unexpected Treasure
*Hidden Treasure
*Holiday Treasure
*Priceless Treasure

Baby for the Billionaire:
*The Tycoon's Revenge
*The Tycoon's Vacation
*The Tycoon's Proposal
*The Tycoon's Secret
*The Lost Tycoon

Surrender:
*Surrender - Book One
*Submit - Book Two
*Seduced - Book Three
*Scorched - Book Four

Forbidden Series:
*Bound -Book One
*Broken - Book Two
*Betrayed - Book Three
*Burned - Book Four

PROLOGUE

"HAVE WE PUSHED Ashton too far?" Richard Storm took a large gulp of good scotch and looked toward the ceiling as he thought about his words.

"What do you mean?" Joseph asked.

"He's not the same man he was a few years ago," Richard said, a heavy sigh showing the even heavier heart inside.

"But the goal was for him to grow up," George pointed out.

"Yes, to grow up, but not to turn into this hard-nosed robot he's become. I barely even recognize my son anymore."

"I hate to admit it, but I agree. I feel like we've all pushed him too hard," Joseph said.

Richard sighed. "He's been busting his ass for four years now trying to prove that he's not just another trust fund baby, that he is worthy of the Storm — and of course Anderson — name. But in that war he's been waging, a piece of his soul has gone missing in action."

"I love that he wants to make you proud, Richard," George told him.

"He wants to make all of us proud, but this isn't what I want. Yes, I'm eager for him to marry and give me grandbabies, but above all, I want him to be happy," Richard said, then realized his glass was empty. "I don't know how much longer I can take this stress."

Richard's two brothers stared at him in concern. The two Anderson patriarchs had been separated from him at birth, and they'd only met decades later, but his pain was their pain. After all, their DNA was almost identical.

"You should look on the bright side, though," George said. "He used to be a devil-may-care bartender, and now he's running a wildly successful business."

Joseph piped in. "And didn't you tell us that he used to be Mr. Playboy, just tomcatting all around both coasts? And now he's engaged to be married. That's another step in the right direction."

"You've met his fiancée," Richard snorted. "Yes, she has a fancy-schmancy name, and makes regular appearances in the society column. But she's really nothing but a gold-digger out for alimony. Wouldn't give him the time of day until she found out about his net worth. Sure, she bats her tinted eyelashes, but she's no prize — unless you want to call her a prize witch."

"But what can we do?" George asked.

"I did what I could. I found the perfect match for Ashton. I gave a card to that lovely woman I mentioned before, Savannah Mills, but she never applied for the job I set up. That was two years ago, and now she has a master's in oceanography. I can't see her taking a job down at the docks after that."

"Oh, yes, I remember that now," Joseph said. "We've been so busy with the other kids, I'd temporarily forgotten. I'm not getting any younger, I'm afraid."

"Do you think we ought to move on from this Savannah?" Richard asked. "She really seemed to be The One, so I hate to give up."

"No," Joseph boomed — that's what he always did. BOOM. "When love is meant to be, it's meant to be. If she just finished her master's and she's set her sights on a PhD, you still have three months before the fall term starts. Maybe now is the perfect time for her and Ashton to finally meet up."

"But he's still got that fiancée of his," Richard growled.

"She won't last," George said. "Think about it. If Ashton sees Savannah, he'll have to make comparisons, and the gold-digger will flame out. Your son isn't that stupid, is he?"

"I wish I could be sure," Richard replied, and a frown took over his face. "As I said, Ashton's track record with women isn't the best. And now, with him trying to prove something to himself or to us, he's making even bigger mistakes."

"Ah, those boys, all of them, know how to put on a mask. I know Ashton has a heck of a lot more soul and a lot more character than he's letting on. Somewhere deep down inside him, the real Ashton is still alive and kicking," Joseph assured them.

"I hope so, brother, because I'm beginning to think that son of mine won't figure it out until it's far too late," Richard said.

Joseph threw him a determined look. "We never give up on the people we love. Sometimes we just have to bring out the electric cattle prod."

Richard finally had a ghost of a smile. "Then let's start planning. I happen to know that Savannah is more intrigued than ever before over sunken treasures. If she can get some free boat rides out to a site where a ship full of treasure is rumored to have sunk, I can see her finally taking that job down at the docks."

"Hmm. Good thing Ashton does private cruises, isn't it?" George said with a laugh.

The three men bent their heads together.

CHAPTER ONE

A BREATHTAKING VIEW OF the Pacific Ocean glimmered before her as Savannah Mills stood at the top of the private docks and gazed at another spectacular sunset.

The scents, sounds, and sights of the West Coast had always filled her with joy. It was unlike anything she'd ever experienced in the whole United States — heck, the entire world, for that matter. Okay, dammit, she'd never traveled beyond these Western Coast states, but who was counting? Completely beside the point. She'd looked at the photos on the Internet, and that had to count for something.

When she began moving forward, she stumbled on the dock, nearly face-planting before she managed to get her balance back. Being a first-class klutz wasn't what she prided herself on, but nobody's perfect.

When she reached the gates barring the way down to the docks on the beautiful Orcas Island outside of Seattle — one of the San Juan Islands — Savanna pressed in the code she'd been given. The gates opened without a hitch.

Maybe Savannah loved the ocean because it was endless. If you were on it, you could run away from the rest of the world, never to be found again — unless you wanted to be. That freedom was priceless to her.

She'd been in school for what felt like forever, so this summer was her break. She was going to resist cracking a single book … nah. She knew herself better than that, and she wouldn't last two weeks on such a ridiculous mission. But still, she was going to make it at least one *single* week. Plus, she was about to begin a dream job for the summer before she was locked away again in the classroom, the lab, and the library.

Yes, she loved school, obviously, or she wouldn't have a bachelor's in biology and a master's in oceanography, and she wouldn't be pursuing a doctorate once three short months passed by. But in the summer all she wanted to feel was fresh wind on her cheeks and seawater lapping over her feet. Did that make her a bad person?

Nope. It made her free. Free of classes, free of homework, free of late-night studying. Free!

She made her way down until she was standing before the boats. Some were smaller than others, but they all were well taken care of, and they all had Sea Storm Enterprise written in bold blue letters across them.

Ha! Catchy, though a bit scary, but since Storm was the owner's last name, it was pretty dang cute. And the owner obviously had *cojones* to use a name like that.

This was a business that catered to those who wanted anything from the best private boating to the experience of a smaller but more luxurious cruise line. And she was now going to be a part of that world for the next three months. She reached out to caress one of the boats … and she was nearly startled into face-planting again.

"Care to tell me what you're doing on these docks?"

A shiver rushed down Savannah's spine at the sound of a deep, dark voice behind her. But after nearly jumping out of her skin, she was immediately tempted to kick herself for her fear. Negative emotions would no longer hold her back, not in this lifetime. She'd had enough of all that.

When she turned, she faced a muscled chest barely hidden from her view underneath a tight button-down white oxford shirt. It took her a little while to lift her head and look into this man's bright blue eyes. Along the way, she hadn't missed his lips, still compelling even if they were pressed together in a scowl.

"Are you mute?" he had the effrontery to ask.

She was instantly ticked off.

"Whoa. That was rude," Savannah said, finding her voice. One hand on her hip, she sent this man a look that had made other males cower before her. No man would speak to her this way again, not as long as she was breathing.

"I'm generally rude to anyone who trespasses on private property — even a woman who obviously thinks that because she's pretty, she can go wherever she damn well pleases."

"I was invited here," she said. "I don't think your boss will be too happy with you when he finds out how you're treating his other employees," she told him with a mocking grin. There was the attitude she'd been searching for.

She refused to let this man belittle or intimidate her. No freaking way. Yeah, he had shoulders that seemed to go on and on, a chest half the size of Texas, plus a chiseled jawline that sculptors would drool over … and she was more than sure he was aware of all that. Why was it that great-looking men thought they owned the whole damned world and could treat other people like dirt? Because they usually did. Whatever. His attitude was *greatly* reducing his attractiveness — in her eyes, at any rate.

His full lips turned up as he took a step toward her, and Savannah felt her heart slam against her rib cage. She stumbled backward a few inches, before she was able to stop herself. Dammit. She wasn't going to retreat.

"And please tell me who hired you. I'd like to pass the information along," he said, coming even closer, way too far into her personal space.

"Mr. Storm," she said. *In your face, pig!*

"Oh, really? You spoke to *Mr. Storm* in person?" the man asked.

What a strange thing to say.

"Yes, as a matter of fact, I did. He approached me at my university and said I was a perfect fit." She felt good in her righteousness. This man was obviously a disgruntled worker. "As a matter of fact, he spoke to me not only once, but twice."

"What did Mr. Storm look like?"

"Why all these questions? I'm sure you know what the boss looks like," she told him.

"I assure you that I do know what the boss looks like. But I'm not so sure you know how to speak the truth."

Man, this guy had something up his nether regions. And who in the world spoke to people this way? Ugh! "Are you accusing me of something?" she asked.

"Isn't that clear?" he said, and he didn't even try to hide the smug smile spreading across his lips. "In case I need to make myself even more clear, I think you're a liar. I don't think you've talked to *Mr. Storm*." He took another step closer. "I also can't figure out what you're doing on these private docks."

"I told you I was hired. Why else would I be here?"

"Because you're after something," he said.

"Do you think I plan on taking off with one of the boats?" she asked him.

"Maybe. Wouldn't be the first time someone tried."

Damn, he was an arrogant ass.

"I've never been so insulted in my life," she snapped.

"I find that hard to believe."

His smirk was insufferable. Savannah almost decided that working on the ocean, as much as she loved the idea, wasn't worth it if it meant dealing with this monstrous man. She glared at him, but she refused to yell. That would give him too much satisfaction. And before she did something as stupid as quitting a job that paid well and provided extra benefits she desperately needed, she took a calming breath.

"I assure you," she said, "that Mr. Storm is going to have words with you." The man she'd met would never want people like this to be the first face a new employee saw. No way. Mr. Storm had been kind and enthusiastic.

There was also no use in continuing this conversation. The man was obviously convinced he was king of the docks. Something he would soon be assured that he was not. He was most likely just a grunt worker with an inflated sense of his importance.

"I somehow doubt that Mr. Storm will be in the least bit upset when you get kicked the hell off these docks," he almost purred. And he reached for her.

Hell, no!

Savannah panicked. She didn't want this man to touch her. She scooted backward ... and quickly realized her mistake, but it was already too late. There was no more dock behind her.

It was funny how she noticed the man's eyes widen as she felt air beneath her foot. She was going down — and it was going to be cold.

CHAPTER TWO

ASHTON STORM FROZE as this mysterious woman fell in what seemed to be slow motion. But the moment she hit the water, he was galvanized, and he immediately kicked off his deck shoes and dived in just as her head popped up against the lapping surface of the ocean.

He reached her within seconds, but he almost wished he hadn't decided to rescue her. She began pushing against him, not to get closer but trying to get away.

She seemed to be something of a swimmer, but the shock of landing in the Pacific Ocean, which was far from warm, had him frightened for her. Would it make her muscles seize up? Would she sink back below the surface? He had to be practical. His ass was on the line and this was a lawsuit waiting to happen. Maybe that had been her plan all along. Women, women, women.

11

"Stop fighting me!" he blurted out after a few moments of struggling with her. She'd been flailing, and she'd hit him in the head more than once.

Surprisingly enough, this wretched woman, a nonentity who hadn't seemed to hear a single thing he'd said up to this point, did what he'd demanded. She said nothing as he pulled her to the ladder and pushed her onto it. He enjoyed the outraged gasp when he gave her a little push — right on her round little ass. Damn, the woman was beyond fine in the rear part of the department store.

When they were both back on the dock, Ashton couldn't help but admire Savannah's long black hair and spitting dark brown eyes. This was no wet-T-shirt contest, but her clothes were plastered to her body anyway. Yep, he could see all she had to offer, and the view was well worth that splash in the ocean.

"Are you happy now?" she growled.

Ashton stopped what he'd been about to say and looked at her in surprise. "You're going to blame me for what happened?"

"You're the one who pushed me into the water. You're obviously nothing more than a ... a ... a bully," she said, and just then her entire body began to shake.

Even though it was an unusually warm June evening, the breeze blowing in off the ocean was very cold.

"I in no way pushed you," he gasped, but he quickly tamped down his outrage. "However, and that's a big *however*, I'll be the better person here — the better man, dammit — and hit the Pause button on this part of the conversation. Let's wait until we get inside to continue our little spat. You need to dry off before you catch a cold." He was telling her that as he began moving up the dock. "Looks like you'll be able to board one of the ships after all. Try not to take it for a test ride."

"A cold is a virus, not something you catch from a dip in water." The woman refused to budge. "Perhaps you mean *hypothermia*. And there's no way I'm going anywhere with you."

"Then leave. I don't really give a damn," he said. Granted, he was bluffing. His curiosity was piqued and he had to know what this woman's story was.

"What?"

"I'm wet and I'm cold. I'm not standing out here arguing with you. If you want to warm up, come inside. If you want to pout like a child, take off."

"Pout? *Pout?*" She rolled her eyes. "Fine! Just give me a towel. I'm sure you people have something like that here on these docks."

"You'll have to follow me to get it," he called back to her, not slowing. But he could hear her footsteps as she trudged reluctantly behind him.

A smile transformed his face as he continued on his way. Something about this woman's attitude intrigued him, and he was having fun. That hadn't happened to him lately.

Striding up to the biggest boat he had in his fleet, the one with his offices on it, he held out his hand to assist her across the ramp.

"I'm fine," she told him, brushing past him and sending a bolt of awareness right to his groin. This wasn't good — not good at all. He was engaged to be married, dammit. But none of that seemed to matter to his lower regions, because he found himself leaning against her. And, heaven forgive him, he began whispering into her ear.

"Yes, you are."

She paused, but only for a millisecond, before she continued moving aboard the exquisitely decorated vessel. He pressed forward past the main dining hall, where up to two hundred and fifty passengers could enjoy meals while socializing.

Top-notch paintings from countries around the world hung on the walls above pieces of antique furniture that Ashton had personally played a part in choosing. He wanted his passengers to have an unforgettable experience, and they always did, leaving his excursions feeling refreshed, pampered, and well-traveled.

Ashton hadn't skimped on costs — the floors were constructed of blond woods from Europe. The ship boasted the finest fabrics, all in rich colors. The fixtures were antique gold, and not a single surface dared carry any grime or even a speck of dust.

"This wasn't what I was expecting," the woman said with a look of awe. "It's stunning."

Her comment actually made him smile, which surprised him. But he was proud of all he'd accomplished in four short years. He couldn't brush off compliments on those hard-won achievements.

"This business caters to those who don't want to be lost in a crowd of three thousand people. The passengers who sail with us are a very exclusive crowd. These ships top out at three hundred guests, but we normally carry fewer than that. There have yet to be any complaints."

"I bet the customers are completely satisfied. Man, this would be a dream come true for me. A ship big enough not to get blown over on a dark and stormy night, yet small enough to get to ports the huge ships can't. Oh, the places you could explore."

"Is that why you want to work here?" he asked as he moved into his office, and he began to unbutton his shirt. He was done with being wet. So why wasn't she watching the show?

"It's why I *am* working here, at least according to Mr. Storm. And, yes, part of it all is that I love the ocean, everything about it, and all the treasures that are hidden beneath the surface," she said before she seemed to realize she wasn't snapping at him. Her shoulders tensed and she looked into his eyes, making him want to take a step back this time. Then she spoke again. "You're probably the type to hold that against me?"

"Don't tempt me, doll," he said, thinking he wouldn't mind holding himself against such a beautiful body. Shaking his head free of thoughts like that, he went through a private door that led to his bathroom. He grabbed two large towels and, moving back out to his office, handed one over to her.

She wrapped it around herself and stood rigidly in front of him. He set his down while he went back to work on the buttons of his shirt. He peeled it away and turned back to face her. Why did this strange woman grow more fascinating by the minute? Hell, by the second. The nanosecond.

"There's a dryer in the next room. Why don't you use the bathroom and get out of those clothes?" he told her. Damnation. Now he had a vivid mental image of her naked.

That wasn't an image he needed in his mind. He was halfway out of his clothes, and what hung out below his waist hardened painfully. He just hoped that he could keep her from noticing what was happening down there.

"No, thanks. I'd rather stay clothed."

"Oh, come on. I'm not going to attack you, woman. I have some restraint. There's a robe hanging on the back of the door."

Their eyes clashed, and hers rounded just a bit. Yeah, she wasn't as haughty as she was trying to make him think she was. Hmm, she definitely appreciated what was now on display. She *was* watching, and he liked it — he *was* a man, after all. But he also admired her restraint. As he reached for the buttons on his pants, she quickly turned around.

"I ... uh ... yeah, I should get out of these clothes," she stuttered.

He just wasn't sure why she suddenly decided to escape. Was it because she was cold or because she was turned on? But without another word she made a dash toward the offered bathroom. And then the door slammed behind her ... and now she was stripping off those sodden clothes and ... This wasn't at all good. But he had to admire the woman's temper. As a matter of fact, he found it almost endearing. Whimpering females had never been his style.

Stepping into another adjoining room, he pulled on a dry pair of pants and a black T-shirt. It was safer for both of them if he had thick denim covering the part of his body still refusing to behave. Granted, the T-shirt was tight, but a man had to do what a man had to do.

A little later, she returned to his office in his oversized robe, and his mouth actually watered. He wondered if she had taken *everything* off. She was clutching her wet clothes, and water was dripping onto the floor. This was fancy wood, but who the hell cared?

He walked up to her, and he had to struggle a bit to wrest the clothes from her hands. He was a good guy, wasn't he? And he took those clothes to his private laundry area, which wasn't far away. When he came back, this woman wouldn't have any more excuses to escape. For at least the next thirty minutes, it was just the two of them.

A lot could happen in such a short time. But that was yet another thought he really didn't want crossing his mind. Dammit!

Once back in his office, he sat on the edge of his desk, hoping to regain at least a minuscule amount of his sanity back — *and* some control over his libido.

So why couldn't he keep himself from baiting this mystery woman?

"We haven't had a proper introduction yet," he finally said with a smile. And he held out his hand. "I'm Ashton Storm."

She looked at him and then around the room.

"Storm?"

"Yep, Ashton, or Ash, as my friends like to call me."

"Are you related to Richard Storm?"

"Most days I'll admit to being his son," he said. He was really enjoying himself now.

"Oh." Her earlier starchy attitude seemed to vanish. "So you're the boss's kid."

"Nope. Try again."

This was beneath him. But why was he having so much fun? Hell, how could he resist? It had all become clear. She was obviously there because of his father, which would explain how she'd had the code to get onto the private docks. On the bright side, at least she wasn't a thief.

"I don't understand," she said.

"What's your name?"

"Savannah Mills. Mr. Storm hired me to work down here this summer. I mean that your father hired me."

"Ah, I see." He smiled at her, noting the intake of her breath and the way her shoulders seemed to tense.

"What do you see?"

"My father is a practiced meddler. He's an expert in the field."

"Mr. Storm, I really don't understand," she said.

But he held up his hand and stopped her.

"First of all, it's my father who's Mr. Storm. I'm Ashton, or Ash. Secondly, I own this company, Savvy."

"Savvy?"

"Your name is too long. If we're going to be working together, I think I'll call you Savvy. You seem somewhat smart."

"You don't know me nearly well enough to give me a nickname, Mr. Storm. I don't appreciate it," she told him firmly.

"Too bad. I don't like wasting my breath," he replied, his eyes narrowing just a bit at her refusal to listen to something as simple as what she should call him. Didn't bode well for an employee of his. "What exactly did my father hire you to do?"

"He didn't tell me my position. He just said that if I wanted a job down here, it was mine. He knew my qualifications. I told him I was happy to do anything."

"Anything?" Oh, the possibilities that were drifting through his mind.

"Within reason, *Mr. Storm*," she said, that fire back in her eyes.

"I like you, Savvy. You entertain me."

"That's not my purpose. I'm a hard worker, and I want to do my job, not worry about sucking up to the boss."

She blushed immediately, and his pants tightened again, just when he'd about gotten his libido under control. Yep, he was a *hard* worker, too. And how he'd love to work her over. He wasn't going to even think about the *sucking* comment.

"Well, we aren't all that formal down here. We're friendly. We work hard, play harder, and give the customers whatever they want," he said with a wink before adding "within reason."

"Then when do I start?"

"How about now?"

"I'm hardly ready to begin now," she replied. "It's late. My clothes are in the dryer. I haven't filled out the proper forms, and I don't know my job description."

"You said you were willing to do *anything*," he reminded her.

"Within reason!" she fired back.

He laughed, not wanting this meeting to end. But he could see she was more than done with wordplay.

"I'll get the paperwork and you can fill it out while the clothes dry. Then be here tomorrow at eight on the dot. I can't stand tardiness."

She looked away before meeting his eyes again, and he could see there was something else. He could also see that she was reluctant to say what it was.

"Tell me what you're thinking, Savvy. I don't like fishing information out of people."

"Um, well, it's that Mr. Storm — I mean your father," she said, just in case he might have forgotten that Mr. Storm was indeed his father. That made him smile again. "He, um, said that there was a place for me to stay here on the docks while I worked this summer."

Ashton's gut turned over at her words. Yes, he had a home away from the San Juan islands, a nice house near Seattle, but during the summer months he spent most of his nights on these docks. Having her that close didn't seem like the brightest idea to him. Not when he was so damn sexually attracted to her. It didn't fit into his plans at all, into the way he'd laid out his life. Laid …

"He did, huh?"

"Yes, he did."

"And where are you currently staying?" Ashton asked.

"I just arrived in Washington earlier today, from California. I don't have a place here yet. I came straight to the docks."

Dang it all! She'd be living right here, then. That was a lot of temptation — especially at night. He wasn't going to share those thoughts, though.

"Well, then, I'd better get you set up."

He moved forward at the same time that she took a step to the side, and he suddenly found himself tangled with her. The two of them fell, but at the last second, Ashton managed to take the brunt of the fall.

But Savvy landed against him, her robe partially opening, giving him a very enticing view of her nicely formed breasts. Dammit. It appeared as if she had taken *everything* off. But he was able to rip his gaze up to her face. *Self-control!*

Screw it. One kiss couldn't hurt anyone, so he grabbed the back of her head … Just then a loud bang sounded on his wall as his office door was thrust against it.

"What in the name of tarnation is going on?"

Both he and Savvy froze, and then they turned in sync to see the woman standing in his doorway.

Ashton recovered quickly. "Hello, Kalli. Perfect timing, as always," he said. He sat up with Savvy in his arms, then scooted her off his lap none too gently and jumped to his feet.

The woman shot a death glare toward Savvy. "Apparently so," she told Ashton in icy tones.

"This is my new employee. We bumped into each other and fell." For some odd reason, he didn't really give a damn that he'd just been caught completely compromised.

"Yes, of course. That's what it looked like," Kalli snapped. To his amazement, though, she quickly regained her composure.

Ashton wasn't quite sure how to take Kalli's reaction. She'd just busted him with another woman and yet she was sauntering toward him with a seductive smile on her outrageously plump lips. If the roles had been reversed, he'd have decked the guy she was with and then walked right out of the room and out of her life.

Dressed impeccably as always in a green Versace outfit that hugged her skin, she wrapped her long arms around his neck and planted a cold kiss on his mouth.

"I missed you, darling. Why don't you introduce us?"

Ashton couldn't seem to find his voice quickly enough, because Kalli turned from him and faced Savvy, who looked like a frightened mouse stuck in a trap.

"Since my fiancé seems to be a little flustered, I'll go ahead and introduce myself. I'm Kallista Blanche Huntington-Hart. Ashton and I are engaged to be married." She held up her hand to show off a gigantic diamond.

"It's nice to meet you, Ms. Hart. I'm Savannah Mills, the newest grunt employee."

There was just enough of a spark in Savvy's eyes for Ashton to see that she wasn't in the slightest bit intimidated by his fiancée. Hot damn if that wasn't sexy too. Double dammit! He couldn't help it, but his opinion of Savvy went up another notch as the three of them stood in his roomy office.

"Hmm. A grunt, huh? I figured."

Instead of responding to that, Savvy turned toward her new boss. "If you can give me those papers, I'll get them filled out and give you two some privacy."

Privacy. Yeah, he looked forward to having some with Savvy. But that might be a bit difficult with his fiancée hanging around. What to do, what to do? Why did life have to be so effing difficult? Especially right after it had become so much better.

Well, then again, adversity only brought out the best in a man, didn't it? *What doesn't kill me ...*

CHAPTER THREE

H E WAS DOING the right thing.

This was his mantra, the one he kept repeating to himself as Kalli continued talking, her fingers waving in the air as she moved around the desk and talked about seating charts and who couldn't be near who — sorry, near *whom* – and other boring-as-hell wedding details.

No. That wasn't something he should be thinking. Kalli was perfect for him, perfect in every sense of the word. She was blue-blooded, sophisticated, beautiful, and respectable. She was the ideal mate for a successful man like himself. She'd keep up appearances and crank out genetically admirable heirs.

She was the sort of wife a man in his position was supposed to marry.

So if that was all true, why in the hell did he keep wandering to his office windows, the ones overlooking the docks, just so he could catch another glimpse of his newest employee. And where did she get off wearing such inappropriate attire?

Even as he thought that, he knew he was being a jerk, and he was also close to getting off. Yes, she was wearing shorts, but so were most of the men and women out there. It was just that he didn't get a hard-on watching his male employees while they walked around in board shorts. Hell, not even when watching the other women.

There was a God after all, he thought, almost smiling.

But Savvy was wearing a pair of shorts that hugged her thighs and showcased the muscles in her calves as she stretched up to scrub the side of one of his boats. As she reached higher, her top crept up and he got an enticing view of her toned midsection.

Damn, one week on the docks and her creamy skin was already getting a nice golden glow to it. It looked good on her — really, *really* good.

"Are you listening to a thing I'm saying, Ashton?"

Kalli's irritated voice pulled him away from those straying thoughts. Turning away from the view and focusing, or trying to, on the woman he was soon to marry, he plastered an unreadable expression onto his face. Yes, he was about to be married, and it would be best — and brightest — to remember that.

"Of course, darling," he told his fiancée. "It's just that we have a lot going on down here at the moment."

"You always have a lot going on, Ashton. But our wedding is important, too," she said with a pout.

Maybe she was trying to be adorable right now, but he could hardly focus on her when the docks were such a hive of activity. That didn't mean he didn't care about his fiancée; it just meant he was a busy man. Good. That thought made him feel better about himself already.

"I agree fully. I'm sorry," he told her. He moved across the room and commanded himself to give his full attention to this beautiful woman, a woman polished in every way.

"Good." Then she began babbling again as she pointed to little squares on the giant piece of paper in front of them.

He lasted only about sixty seconds before his head was turning back toward the windows. How much longer was this going to take?

"Okay," she said, "I think that takes care of the seating."

Great! This was all done. He'd been able to keep his eyes open during the bit about who was to sit where during the upcoming ordeal — or ordeals, to get technical.

"Now we'll look at food."

No, of course it wasn't done. She grabbed his hand and led him over to another table in his office, and he saw a giant notebook sitting there. Damn, elopement was sounding better and better by the moment. But Kalli would never be okay with that. Sigh.

"I've finalized the reception menu. Javier has outdone himself, I'll have you know," she said with a high-pitched laugh.

Why hadn't he ever noticed how annoying that sound was? But as soon as that thought came to him, he shook his head. There was something seriously wrong with him today. He had to remind himself again what a great catch this high-society woman was.

"Why don't we stop planning for a few minutes?" he asked as he reached for her, pulling her against his body.

"Ashton, I have an appointment in one hour. We have to get as much done as possible," she told him, pushing against his hold.

"It can wait."

He leaned down and kissed her, urging his body to respond, to feel passion, heat. Finally, she reached up, wrapped her hands around his neck and pressed against him. After a few moments, he released her mouth.

"That was lovely," she said before tugging against him again.

This time he let her go. Dammit! There had to be something seriously wrong with him, because Kalli was flawlessly beautiful. He had no idea whether everything was real, but it was definitely spectacular.

And he hadn't even managed to get an inkling of an arousal with that kiss.

Kalli opened the wedding planning book, and Ashton found himself wandering back over to the window. What he saw certainly stirred his blood far more than that kiss just had. Savvy was still out there, and she seemed to be sidling up to one of his men, flaunting all her charms. If he had anything at all to do with it — and he did — it was going to stop.

"I'm going to have to cut this meeting short, my ... my love. It appears as if there's a problem on the docks," he said. He had to fight to prevent his anger from showing in his voice.

Just then Kalli's phone went off. Talk about being saved by the bell. Or the ringtone. Whatever.

"That works out well, Ashton, because that's my mother texting. The appointment was moved up."

Within seconds, she was packed up and walking away. Ashton stayed where he was, gazing out the window. He wanted his temper to cool down a bit, and he definitely wanted his fiancée gone before he went outside.

CHAPTER FOUR

"I MIGHT HAVE TO admit that nothing is worth this grunt work. Not finding treasure, not working on the ocean, not getting my PhD. *Nothing*."

Grumbling as she stretched on her tiptoes to clean the side of the boat, Savannah almost slipped and took another nosedive into the cold Pacific Ocean. For once, her klutzy limbs didn't fail her, though, and she managed to stabilize herself.

But she really hated ladders, and she knew only too well that falling into the water would be even worse the higher up she was. Basic physics plus an earlier experience this week. Luckily, the boss hadn't been around for that little mishap, her second plunge into the brine. She was tired, sore, and more than ready to give this up and go back to the library.

But, no, she had never been a quitter, and she wasn't about to start now. No way, no how. Plus, this was good. She'd put on about ten pounds in the last couple of years which she wasn't too happy about. Working on the docks this summer should help her shed that extra weight in no time at all.

There. She'd managed to find the end of the rainbow, the pot of gold and all that. And she felt much, *much* better about it. This was a workout she was getting paid to do. Yay for her.

"You know you're working entirely too hard," a co-worker told her. "The boss is tied up for at least the next few hours. I saw his aristocratic bride-to-be bringing in the *big* book of wedding planning."

"I saw that. But just because Mr. Storm isn't watching, that doesn't mean I'm going to slack off," she told the fellow.

"I say we take a little dive into the water and cool off — and then warm back up … at my place." Weston said this with a giant wink.

Her co-worker had been flirty since she'd joined the crew. As a matter of fact, most of the men were pretty dang open with their catcalls. Plus their sexual double entendres had been less than subtle. But the guys were generally harmless. Weston, on the other hand, had made it beyond clear that he wouldn't mind a romp in the sack.

He was about her age, and he'd been giving her the eye and putting the moves on her ever since she'd arrived on the docks. She really wished she felt something for him — he was great-looking, with sun-kissed blond hair, *Miami Vice* stubble on his jaw, and twinkling blue eyes. He was also tall — who didn't love that in a male? — *and* he had a smile that could replace the sun.

But so far, the man hadn't inspired her to actually accept a date. Dang it!

"I think it's safer if I just finish my work so I can take a long shower and then make it out to my deck to stargaze later tonight while I drink a beer."

"Don't most women prefer wine?" he asked, edging a little closer.

"I don't do stereotypes," she informed him. "And after a hot day, nothing tastes as good as an icy-cold beer from a can."

"But you can always suck harder from a bottle," he told her with yet another wink.

Savannah couldn't help it. She burst out laughing. If she'd actually felt threatened by the man, it would be an entirely different story, but she knew she was safe. Sure, he'd like to date her, and bed her, but his pride wasn't wounded when she turned him down.

"I wonder why you're still single, Weston, with suave lines like that," she finally said as she patted his arm.

"Is this a brothel, or do either of you actually do any work?"

Savannah froze. *Crap.* Just what she needed right now — to be busted by the boss. She threw a quick but savage look to Weston, who'd told her only a little while ago that the boss would be tied up for hours. Her co-worker had been wrong. Weston just winked for the third time and scampered off, out of the line of fire. Traitor!

Now she was alone with Ashton and something was wrong. Big surprise.

"Yes, Mr. Storm. I have been working, as you can see," she said. "However, the longer you stand here scowling at me, the longer it's going to take for me to do what I'm being paid to do."

He seemed taken aback by her boldness. Why was that? Hadn't he seen it at their first meeting? She did her best to be sociable, but she did have a backbone, and it was almost always in evidence now. She'd grown it from the fists of her father and from her years of study. She wasn't going to be pushed around anymore. That time was over.

"Did you happen to forget that I'm your boss? If I need to speak to you, don't you think it wise to listen?"

"Of course, Mr. Storm." She could play the obedient little employee if that was the role he wanted her to play. But he'd better not expect her to cower. That would be asking far too much.

"Good. Now come with me. Some of your forms are incomplete."

He turned, and once again the man had no doubt that she was going to follow him. And there was no reason for doubt. She had to do what he wanted and that was the advantage he held over her. But she couldn't stay completely silent.

"Shouldn't I tell Tom? He'll wonder why I'm not on the job."

"It's been taken care of," he replied, and he didn't slow his stride.

Savannah had to fight to keep herself from exploding. Dang it. This man wasn't really doing anything any other boss wouldn't do. But the two of them hadn't gotten off to a great start, and she certainly knew how to hold on to a grudge.

She promised herself that she'd work on that.

When they stepped into his office, Savannah's eyes immediately went to the spot on the floor where they'd been tangled up less than a week ago. No, nothing had actually happened. The two of them had fallen into each other. Nothing more. He hadn't been about to kiss her. That had all been in her head.

Okay, she could lie to herself all she wanted, but she'd seen the look in his eyes. It wasn't as if she'd never been kissed before. She had — plenty of times!

Who in the heck was she kidding? She'd been kissed a few times, and the first one hadn't been until her freshman year of college. That kiss had sucked. The next few guys hadn't gotten much better.

So she bailed out. Why fool around with college boys, at least until she at least found a guy who lit her on fire? That had yet to happen. Sure, she'd had plenty of opportunity. College guys were just plain horny, ready to rock all around the clock. But she didn't want her first time to be with some drunken frat boy who stuck it in her and then fell asleep with her pinned beneath him.

It wasn't asking too much to hold out for more, was it?

And even though her boss had stirred more feelings in her in the span of a few minutes than any other man — or boy — ever had, she was *not* going to act on that. The man had a fiancée, after all. And Savannah was determined never to be a homewrecker.

If only she could convince herself to quit lusting after him. It was hormones. That's all it was. She knew science, and she could get over this.

"Are you going to answer my question?"

Ashton's voice snapped her out of her daze. Wow. He was irritated.

"I'm sorry. I missed what you said." Embarrassment heated her cheeks. Only one thing saved her pride — that he had no clue where her mind had just been. If he knew, she'd have to quit right then and there.

"I said that I'm going to start training you to be able to go out on our cruises. I'm short-staffed in that department right now, and I expect all crew members to know their cruise jobs inside and out. Within a month, if you do well, you'll be able to go on a voyage. Are you interested?"

"Oh, yes, yes, for sure," Savannah told him, elated at the possibility of hitting the ocean. "When does the cruise leave? Which ship are we taking? Where is it going?" She fired questions off without giving him a chance to answer.

"Most likely our Alaskan voyage, where we stop in Sitka, Glacier Bay, Kodiak, and Dutch Harbor before heading back home. I'll have someone train you for the main ship when their schedule frees up for them to do so. This is where we have approximately two hundred and fifty guests on board. You would work the cleaning crew."

"I've cleaned before. It won't be a problem. What about free time? Do we get any?" she asked, then thought that sounded clumsy and decided to clarify. "I didn't mean that I don't appreciate the job opportunity or that I won't work hard. But I love cruising the seas, and I'm excited about going to new places, really getting to see them."

"You'll work specific hours. The rest of the time, barring emergencies, you will have plenty of free time."

"How long are we in each port?"

"Since we limit our stops, we're normally in each place for two days and one full night. We cruise overnight to each new location."

"Thank you for this opportunity, Mr. Storm. I promise you I won't mess it up," she told him. She was beyond ecstatic, and without thinking, she jumped over to him and threw her arms around his neck. "You don't know how much this means to me."

Big mistake. She realized it the nanosecond her arms were around Ashton's neck. But before she was able to pull away, he was clasping his hands behind her back and drawing her against him.

"I'm so sorry," she gasped. "I don't know what I was thinking."

"I happen to like this impulsive, affectionate Savvy," he said, not allowing her to escape.

Panic set in. She couldn't allow him to do a repeat tango with her on his office floor. Why didn't she think before acting? She'd been asking herself this for a very long time.

"Well, it's inappropriate," she told him, tugging against his hold again.

This time he let her go. She took several steps back and did her best to create as much distance between them as humanly possible.

"How so?" he said, an obvious challenge.

First she sputtered at him. Then she did what she always did when she got overstressed. She closed her eyes for a few seconds, counted to ten, then took a cleansing breath. When she reopened her eyes, he was looking at her strangely, but he hadn't moved. That was good.

"Did you forget that you have a fiancée?" Wow. Her voice was calm, rational. She was very proud of herself.

"What does that have to do with our sharing a moment together with a friendly hug?"

"Oh, you are so smooth, aren't you, Ashton?" She didn't even think about her slip of using his first name. "Is that how you justify cheating? Do you say that it started out friendly, and then that somehow things got out of hand? Are you really *that* guy?"

His eyes narrowed the longer she spoke. She was ticking him off. Good. She'd rather have him mad at her than lusting after her. Especially when she wasn't immune to his charm.

"Are you finished, Savvy?" He was eerily calm. She nodded. "Fine. Now it's my turn to speak. Yes, I find you attractive, and, yes, I can see us setting off some fireworks in the bedroom. But, no, I don't cheat, not ever."

"So you weren't about to kiss me the other day?" She decided she wasn't going to back down. It was better to get it all out on the table now.

"Yes, I was. But I would have stopped at that."

"Are you proud of that?" She was beginning to lose some of her cool all over again.

"It was just going to be a little kiss," he said, as if she were being unreasonable. "No biggie."

"So you wouldn't care if your fiancée shared a *little* kiss with another man?" she asked.

His reaction wasn't what she'd expected.

"You know what?" he said, his lips twitching. Then he waited.

"What?" she finally demanded.

"I don't think I would."

He took a step toward her, and that's when Savannah decided she'd better cut her losses and get the hell out of there. She'd been strong. She'd said what she needed to say, but now it was time to go.

There was the real possibility that she was going to get out on the ocean. And she wanted to be on that boat when the next cruise sailed. So there wouldn't be any more goading of her boss. That meant she needed to stay at least twenty yards from him at all times.

Shouldn't be too hard.

CHAPTER FIVE

THERE WERE VERY few times when Savannah actually wanted a beer. For the most part she *was* a wine drinker, though she hadn't been about to admit that to Weston — and when the day had been just a bit too much, a nice cocktail hit the spot. But beer was only for special occasions.

A beer was great when the sun was out and the heat scorching. The flavor just burst in her mouth at that point. Also at baseball games. She had to have a hot dog covered in relish and mustard, plus a light beer to wash it all down. And for some reason she loved a cold one on New Year's Day. That was a bit problematic, because it was winter outside then, and she'd normally drunk a few cocktails the night before. So the other times made sense, but she wasn't sure about the first of January. Oh, wait! She was far from an alcoholic, but that probably fell into hair-of-the-dog territory.

Today had been a scorcher — beyond a scorcher actually, topping out at ninety-three with too much humidity in the air and not enough wind from the ocean. It was normally in the nice and cool seventies this time of year on the islands off of Washington state.

Not now. And it was just her luck, wasn't it? Especially when her crappy boss had her doing crappy ass work, to use a technical term. But there was a positive ending to all the sweat and curse words that had dripped from her this afternoon. Yep. It was a nice, icy-cold, fully refreshing Corona Light with just a little lemon. Sometimes she wanted a can, and sometimes a bottle. Just depended on what brand she was drinking.

Sitting in a comfortable lounge chair on the upper deck of the boat she was living in, she could watch the stars grow brighter in the skies, and hear the waves crashing against the shore. It didn't get any better than this.

That was until her bottle was empty and then, in place of the soothing sounds of the ocean, she was hearing raised voices — and they were coming nearer and nearer.

Savannah knew that she should climb down the ladder and go below deck into her private room. But that's not what happened. After all, she had to be careful around those ladders. She dropped from her chair, flattened herself out against the flooring, and peeked between the slits to watch as Ashton strode down the docks with a very irate Kalli on his heels.

And on her own heels too. As Kalli continued screaming, one of the woman's inappropriately high heels — at least inappropriately high for a dock with large cracks in between each board — got caught, and down she went, straight to her well-bred knees. Splat!

And it looked painful.

"Ashton!"

That wasn't love in her tone. Ashton looked back at his fiancée and paused. The two of them were far too close to Savannah's boat now. If either of them turned, they would spot her.

She backed up a bit, but dang it, this was better than a soap opera, and she just didn't want to leave. She knew she should —

knew Ashton was going to be pissed if he caught her eavesdrop-
ping — and yet she kept on spying. Cable was expensive and this
was free.

"Get over here and help me up," Kalli called out.

"I warned you not to wear those heels on the docks," he said
impatiently. But he moved back toward her.

"What else was I supposed to do? I couldn't wear flats to a
show, could I?" Kalli was no longer screeching. Her voice was
now quavering, as if she were fighting tears.

Savannah was almost feeling sympathy for this woman. Where
that was coming from, she just didn't know. But if she ever had
the opportunity to go to a show, well, she'd want to dress up too.
She hated to admit it, but she could almost see the other woman's
point of view.

"You could have brought a change of shoes, Kalli."

"And you didn't need to bring me back here instead of to your
nice place outside Seattle, which was much nearer to the show,"
his fiancée countered as she took his hand and wobbled to her
feet. "This is ruined now!" she snapped, holding up the broken
shoe in her free hand.

"Sorry," he said, though he didn't sound sorry at all.

"Dammit, Austin Daniel Storm. Do you know how much
these shoes cost?"

"I'm sure they cost a lot. Are you done with your tantrum,
or do I need to continue to act like I give a damn about a pair of
overpriced shoes? Especially shoes that really don't do that much
for you."

He said the words with no inflection, as if he were having a
polite conversation. It took Savannah a moment to realize he was
insulting the woman he was intending to marry. Apparently, it
took Kalli a moment to realize it too.

But when she did, the rage on the woman's face was obvious.
She yanked her hand away from Ashton's and took several stilted
steps back, one heel on, one off.

"You know what, Ashton? You can go find some oil and ... use
that big hand of yours on yourself tonight." With that, she lurched

around and headed back up the docks. She'd refused to shed the unbroken shoe, but she was limping along as quickly as she could.

"I'll probably have a better time," Ashton mumbled. "It's been weeks anyway since I've slept with you," he muttered too softly for Kalli to hear, but just loud enough for Savvy to catch every word.

Savannah almost laughed out loud, but she suppressed it. That would certainly get her caught. Still, a squeak escaped her mouth, and, damn her luck, Ashton looked in her direction. With superhuman speed, she jerked backward, barely managing to catch herself. She'd almost pitched over the ladder right behind her.

She lay back as flat as she could, not daring to move an inch. But she couldn't help but listen for any possible sound to alert her that Ashton had moved on.

Without knowing how much time had passed after her triple axel, she finally decided she was either going to move or freeze out there on the deck. But just as she began to get up, she was given another fright.

"Enjoy the show?"

So much for her acrobatic skills. Klutzy acrobatic skills. She'd been busted.

CHAPTER SIX

HEART THUNDERING, SHE flopped over onto her back and stared straight up at the intimidating figure that Ashton made. And at the moment, he wasn't even trying to scare her — or she didn't think he was. She'd managed to avoid the man for a few days, but now that it was after midnight with absolutely no one around, he decided it was a good time for a chat. Of course, it didn't help that he'd caught her snooping in on him.

If she'd just gone below deck the way she should have when the whole brouhaha began, she wouldn't be in this awkward position right now — literally and figuratively.

Then, Ashton shocked the heck out of her when he suddenly dropped to the deck and lay down next to her. She tensed wondering what to do. She'd never been in a position like this before.

"I wasn't spying or anything," she finally said when the silence was almost deafening.

"Give me a break. Sure you were. But in your defense, I would have done the same if I'd been in your position."

He didn't seem angry — amused was more like it. She hadn't been expecting that. But she didn't know this man, didn't know him at all, and didn't want to. So how could she judge what sort of mood he was going to be in?

"Okay, fine, I can admit I was watching the show, and it could probably win an Emmy if someone was smart enough to tape it. However, I hadn't set out to do it. I was sitting here, just drinking a nice cold beer and looking at the stars, when you and your fian-cée began making a screen-worthy ruckus. What was I supposed to do? Interrupt my night and run and hide? Go below deck be-cause you and that woman of yours were squabbling? I wasn't ready to do that yet."

She was blathering. She always blathered when she was really nervous. But even knowing that, she sometimes found it impos-sible to stop, dang it.

"And what was up with the shoe situation, Ashton? I mean, really! I would have been upset too if I'd broken a favorite pair of shoes, but then again, I wouldn't wear heels on a dock either..." Oh, please. Just shoot her now. At least she hadn't added that those shoes were fugly as sin.

"Are you planning on torturing me, Savvy? Death by words?" He was laughing as he spoke.

Savannah thought for a moment, and then she really did see the humor. Instead of huffing and puffing, she joined in the laughter, and suddenly the tension was gone.

How could this man be so stiff and formal one moment, and then so carefree the next? She was confused. Up to this point, she hadn't once seen him so ... so friendly.

"You know," he said, "it would be only polite to offer your guest a beer. You *were* the one who mentioned the subject." And he looked as if he were about to get really comfy.

"I'm technically *your* guest, Mr. Storm, as you've already pointed out. You own the boat, and so, by your way of thinking, you should jump up and get us both one," she told him boldly.

He turned his head to look at her for a moment and then shocked her again when he hopped to his feet and moved to the built-in fridge. The man actually grabbed a couple of beers, twisted the tops off, grabbed the slices of lemon she had already cut, and wedged a couple pieces in each bottle.

She finally sat up on the decking, then jumped to her feet before getting back on the lounge chair. That was a major relief — deck floors weren't exactly built for comfort.

"Thanks," she murmured as he handed her a fresh bottle of Corona. She leaned back, took a sip, and then went back to searching the stars. She'd enjoyed looking for shapes in them ever since she was a small child.

"You're welcome, Savvy. I'm enjoying the company."

She stared at him for a moment and chortled. "How in the world are you enjoying my company? It seems we're sniping at each other every chance we get."

"You know what they say, don't you? There's a thin line between love and hate."

She snapped her head back to look at him, then felt tremendous relief when he winked.

"You really like throwing me all out of kilter, don't you?"

"Yes, as a matter of fact, I do." The guy had no qualms about admitting it.

"Do you do that to everyone?" she asked. It wasn't like she was special or anything.

"Not everyone," he said, making her stomach flutter. "Just the people I like."

What in the heck was that supposed to mean? She definitely wasn't opening that door.

"Maybe you should find some more friends, because I'm not all that likable," she told him with a laugh, but it wasn't quite merry enough to cover the reality of those words. "I can be a bit prickly."

"*Prickly*? Don't get me to thinking in those terms, Savvy. And I can't imagine that anyone on this earth would find you unlickable — I mean ... unlikable." He paused to relish her dramatic blush. "You're beautiful, smart, hardworking, and easy to talk to. I'm sure you have a line of people clamoring for your attention. As a matter of fact, Weston seems to hunt you out every chance he can get." He'd added that last part with the slightest of growls.

It took her a while to answer, but it was so lovely to have someone to talk to, someone to share with.

"Sometimes ... life can be quite lonely. Perhaps it's only when a person is really intent. I've been in school so long that it feels like I haven't had a break in ... forever. I do love my little sister more than words could possibly describe, but as for friends — well, I just haven't had time for that."

"You have a sister?" he asked.

"Yes, it's the reason I transferred here. The school has a great program and I get to be with my sis."

"Where is she?" he asked.

"She's been doing medical work in Africa, but she'll be back in a couple of days now." Savannah couldn't wait.

"Hmm. Interesting," he said. Of course, it was interesting. Alexa was the sister everyone liked. But before Savvy was able to say something about that, he spoke again. "Is she anything like you?"

Savannah didn't quite know how to take that question. Was it good? Bad? Should she tell him her sister wasn't available? Though, technically she was, but the thought of Alexa and Ashton dating sent slivers of jealousy running along her spine. But that was stupid. Savannah had no claims on Ashton and she didn't want to. She was just upset about the idea because the man already had a fiancée.

"We're somewhat alike, but Alexa has one of those bubbly personalities that everyone is drawn to. She's amazing."

He paused for a moment, and she would have paid everything in her small savings account to know what he was thinking. Not that it mattered, she tried telling herself.

"You have a —" Ashton stopped whatever he was about to say because of the look that Savvy had just sent him.

She picked things up from here. "You don't get to be bubbly all the time when you're working as hard as I am for a good future. I'm not an old maid, though, if I may use an outdated sexist term. I have plenty of time in life to 'let down my hair' — quote unquote — and giggle all night and day." She knew she was being overly sensitive, but she was always told she was the boring and more uptight sister. Despite the occasional beer. That got old after a while.

He was silent for a moment and then he was even smarter when he changed the subject. "Didn't you make friends in college?"

"Not really. I joined a lot of study groups — one of those high-achieving things — but then I'd move on to the next class. And because I didn't like to go out and party and stuff like that, people quickly lost interest in me. I never really hooked up with anyone."

Savannah blushed again, fiercely, when she thought about what the phrase *hook up* meant now. But she went ahead. "I've always been a little jealous of people who constantly manage to draw other people to them. Then again, if I cared so much, I guess I'd put more effort into it."

"We all need people in our lives, Savvy. We aren't meant to be alone." Ashton reached out his hand and rested it on hers.

Ding ding ding ding! Bad, bad, bad. The red flags were bursting in the air, but the mixed metaphors didn't quite register in her mind. She was all absorbed in the tingling that shot through her at the innocent touch. Of course it was innocent. And this wasn't where this conversation should be leading right now. She gazed desperately at the shapes in the sky.

"Did you know that ancient mariners used the stars when they navigated?" she asked.

His hand stayed on hers, and her heart raced, but she was trying to think of something else to say when he finally spoke.

"Yes. But I never did too much research on it, Savannah, to tell you the truth. I'm more in tune with modern technology."

"I've always been fascinated by anything that has to do with the ocean, and the stars are a big map in the sky, so obviously I've studied them. You can always find your way back home if you just look up." Her throat was beginning to dry out the longer he touched her. Not good at all.

"Do you always speak so much when you're unsettled, Savvy?" he asked, his fingers dancing on her skin.

Okay, now it was time to go. Her heart was racing, her skin tingling, and her throat practically closing. She wasn't sure what she was feeling, but whatever it was, it wasn't good.

"Well, it's been fun, but I'm exhausted," she said with an exaggerated yawn as she sat up, downed the rest of her beer, and practically bounded to her feet.

Big mistake. She immediately began feeling wobbly.

But Ashton leapt up and caught her before she went down. Like a classic romantic hero. And then they were standing there, her gaze held by his, the stars shining in all their glory right over them. She couldn't remember why kissing this man was such a bad idea.

And then she wasn't allowed to think anymore. He was leaning forward and … and … and. Damn. Yes, she knew this wasn't supposed to happen, or she must have known it somewhere deep down inside, but as his lips brushed against hers, as his hands caressed her back, and as his tongue slipped inside her mouth, she couldn't remember anything, let alone why she shouldn't kiss her boss.

His hands slid up and down her back, his lips coaxed hers open, his tongue performed magic, and all the while she was helpless to do anything but cling tightly to him.

"Savvy," he moaned before he trailed his lips down her jaw and sucked the skin of her neck.

Never had she enjoyed a kiss so much. Heck, she'd never experienced anything like this before. Not once! How was she supposed to stop something that felt so right — so incredible? With the other guys, it had been easy to put an end to it because she hadn't felt this heat pooling in her stomach, hadn't felt the rest of the world fade away.

With Ashton, she forgot her own name, and she also forgot the reasons she shouldn't allow him to make her feel such unbelievable passion. The night was made for romance. When his mouth reached the swell of her breast, she somehow gained back her sanity.

"Ashton, stop."

Was that her voice? It didn't sound like her, not at all. It was husky, and breathy, and the moan that followed certainly didn't sound like something from a woman who was really saying no.

"Why?" he groaned before his hand slipped below her shirt.

She pulled back. He let her. Much to her ... hell, her disappointment. Maybe she wanted him to take this decision — not that it was anything rational now — out of her hands. No. She didn't want that. Maybe she thought she did for the moment, but she'd hate herself in the morning.

And finally she managed to speak. "Because you aren't mine."

With that, she turned and walked away. He let her. Savvy didn't sleep well that night, not well at all. The little sleep she did manage to get was filled with dreams of Ashton.

CHAPTER SEVEN

WHAT IN THE freaking universe had he been thinking?

He was engaged to another woman. He wouldn't be a cheater. He'd never cheated before. Sure, he hadn't been in a committed relationship before, so he'd never really been tested, but that was beside the point.

The point was that Kalli was the perfect wife. She was blue blood at its finest. She was literate, funny — at times, anyway — conservative, and the perfect choice to produce children who would make his father and his uncles proud.

Ashton had spent enough years being the bartending playboy. It was his duty now to grow up and act like a Storm. And he had the added responsibility of knowing he wasn't only a Storm but also an Anderson. Damn, that was a lot of weight on a regular guy's shoulders.

So he couldn't mess this thing up with Kalli. He wouldn't do yet another thing that would prove his father right. The old man had pulled him and his brothers and his sister into a room and threatened to take everything away from them. He'd said that they were all spoiled, and that they all needed a purpose in life. And after the initial shock, Ashton had done his damnedest to demonstrate that a man could change. He'd done that.

But he was now playing with fire, whatever that meant nowadays, and that wasn't acceptable.

He didn't want to be a man people couldn't trust. To "party on" and to live life to the fullest was one thing. Or two things. Who was counting? To have no morals at all was completely different. So he had two options. He needed to get rid of the temptation — which was one Savannah Mills — or he needed to learn some self-control and do what he knew was right.

Getting rid of Savvy would be much easier. Dammit. His life had become complicated the moment she'd stumbled onto his docks, and he didn't like "complicated." He liked smooth sailing — on and off the water. But when had he ever taken the easier way when it wasn't a way he wanted to travel? Never that he could think of.

Well, it was too late to do anything more about it tonight, so it wouldn't do him any good to waste time dwelling on the subject. But as he lay in bed, Ashton began getting annoyed. Who in the blazes was this Savannah person to come in and mess up his perfectly laid-out plans for the future? He'd been happy with Kalli. No, not ecstatic. He wasn't deeply in love with her, but he'd been comfortable. He'd never wanted love, really, never wanted someone to hold him down. He'd seen where that could lead. And the end of the road wasn't pretty.

Love brought with it a deep responsibility. You had to make sure that someone else's life was better with you in it than it had been without you. He didn't want to be responsible for anyone else, didn't want that pressure.

And he'd been perfectly content to marry Kalli. She didn't make him uncomfortable, with the exception of that shoe thing, and he'd had decent sex with her. She wasn't someone he got all giddy about inside, but that wasn't what he wanted.

And now, in less than two weeks, Savvy had come along and turned his life into tatters. Who did she freaking think she was? He had half a mind to storm over to her boat — no, not her boat, *his* boat — and give her a piece of his mind. Or a piece of something.

No, not in his best interest. Obviously. But he wasn't exactly sure what *was* in his best interest. He had a clue, though, that the first step in being a hell of a lot healthier was to avoid his newest employee.

He could do that. He was certain of it.

Closing his eyes, Ashton spent the rest of the night tossing and turning. When the sun began rising and he wandered out onto his deck just in time to find Savvy sauntering along the dock and showing off that amazing derrière of hers, he sent a withering look her way. What in the world was she doing dressing the way she dressed?

"Savvy," he hollered, making her whirl around. She'd obviously thought she was alone, and anyone with any real savvy knew that assumptions brought disaster. Or dis-ASS-ter.

Reluctance seemed to follow every step she took toward him, and that only put him in a worse mood. His mood hadn't started out too well to begin with. She was about to receive the brunt of it. Or, in other words, she was cruising for a metaphorical bruising.

"You slacked off yesterday. Don't let it happen again or I'll be left with no choice but to replace you."

Her mouth dropped, and she was obviously trying to figure out where this *Dr. Jekyll and Mr. Hyde* attitude was coming from. Why hadn't he been able to stop himself?

"I don't understand, Mr. Storm. I did everything you told me to do," she finally said.

He couldn't even stop himself now. "You're moving too slowly, *Ms. Mills*. Other people shouldn't have to pick up after you. Do you know what I'm going to say next?"

"I have an idea. 'Shape up or ship out'?"

"Got it in one."

"I find that offensive."

Her irritation, which was now matching his own, didn't bother him in the slightest. He'd rather have her irritated than hurt. For some reason he couldn't stand the thought of hurting her, which was ridiculous.

"I find it offensive when people don't do their job."

She gasped at him, but he decided he'd caused enough damage for now. With a minor snort, he walked away without giving her another chance to respond. But he'd be damned sure to keep tabs on her work.

Maybe she'd give him a reason to fire her. If only the thought of doing just that didn't turn his stomach. *Dammit! Dammit! Dammit!* He kept using that word. But this woman was trouble. He'd known it from the first moment they'd met. And he still knew it.

And yet he didn't appear to be doing anything at all about it. That made him a fool, and that made him seriously unhappy.

Damn them both.

CHAPTER EIGHT

WHO WAS THIS guy? One moment he was carefree and laughing, joking, making out with her — okay, maybe she shouldn't think about that last thing. But the next minute he was yelling at her and stern and threatening her job. She couldn't figure him out.

One thing she knew for sure, though, was that Ashton loathed her now. Savannah felt it in every fiber of her being. Some days he didn't, but right now, he positively loathed her. She'd been working for him for two weeks and he had her doing every disgusting job known to man — and then some jobs probably unknown to anyone but the grunts of the world. And there were a lot of them.

At least she was finally sleeping well. The water rocked her into a deep sleep each night. Well, if she had to be precise, she meant that she was lulled to sleep on the nights she didn't have intimate conversations with Ashton when he changed back from the nice Dr. Jekyll into the scary Mr. Hyde.

And so what if she was doing this sort of menial stuff? She could do any work as long as she got to be on the water. And if the stars all aligned just right, she was going to be out on the ocean on a beautiful cruise going to ports she'd never been to before. That kept her much more perky as she ran the large net through the water, picking up garbage that was floating in.

"Are you enjoying yourself?"

Savannah jumped when she heard the boisterous voice behind her. And she was mortified as she wiped sweat from her brow.

"Hi, Mr. Storm. What are you doing down here?" she asked.

He was with two men who looked so much like him. Interesting.

"Aww, sweetie, why so formal?" Richard said, and he surprised her when he pulled her into a bone-crushing hug.

"I, uh, I ..." She didn't know how to finish.

"Call me Richard," he told her. "I insist. And these handsome young men are my brothers, Joseph and George."

"It's a pleasure to meet you both," she said, touched by their winning smiles.

"Not as much of a pleasure as it is for us," said Joseph, who was the next to give her a bear hug. George then stepped in and swept her into his arms too, and Savannah didn't know what to think. Her ribs might be cracked — a definite possibility. Were they trying to kill her with kindness? She wasn't all that small, but these men were giants.

"Let's take a lunch break," Richard told her. "I'm starving."

"Oh, I can't go right now. I have to finish clearing this water."

"Nonsense," Joseph said. "Everyone needs a break."

"What are you three doing down here?"

The sound of Ashton's voice sent a shiver down Savannah's spine, as it always did, but she was getting much better at covering it up. She didn't even turn to make eye contact with him this time. *Take that.*

"We're here to visit with Savannah," Richard said to his son. "By the way, I don't understand why you have her scooping up garbage. The woman has a master's degree, for goodness sake."

Savannah's cheeks flamed up.

"I wasn't complaining," she assured her boss, finally looking at him. Dang it. Yep. There was the zap, the electricity, that she'd been trying to avoid.

"Is there something wrong with a good day's work?" Ashton asked her sharply.

"I just said I don't have a problem," she snapped. "Of course, *you've* always done a good day's work, haven't you?"

The glare he sent her should have been intimidating. Instead, all it did was make her want to push him into the water that she was busy cleaning up. But then that would just be another piece of garbage she had to scoop back out. Before he was able to answer her, Richard intervened.

"This woman has too much class to complain," Richard informed his son. "I'm the one who thinks her being out here in the hot sun doing menial tasks is a waste of her talents."

"Sorry if you feel that way, Dad, but I've done my fair share of crap work," Ashton told him.

Richard's eyes bored into his son. "And do you still?" he asked. "And were you always that engaged in hard work? I seem to remember ..."

Savannah was curious about this change in topic. She really didn't know much about Ashton. Was his dad insinuating that he'd once been lazy? Now that the focus was getting off her, the conversation was much more interesting.

"I remember too," Ashton said. But he obviously wasn't going to mention his attitude toward work in his trust fund years, at least not in front of Savannah.

"Then let's see it," George told his nephew. "If you help get this dang task done, we can take Savannah to lunch."

Ashton stared daggers at the three men before turning and shooting Savannah a warning look. She just gazed back in an *I-can't-stop-this* expression.

"Go to lunch," he growled. "They won't lay off me unless you do."

"I'm perfectly fine doing my job," she told her tormenter. "I don't expect special treatment."

Ashton took a step closer. "I said, '*Go to lunch*,' Savvy. Do you have a problem with following orders?"

"No, boss, of course not." Savannah probably couldn't have injected any more sarcasm into her voice if she'd tried.

"Good." He turned to walk away.

"We're taking one of your boats over to Orcas Island and eating at the Loft at Madrona," his father said. "You'll join us, son, and captain the ride, of course." Richard took Savannah's arm and threaded it through his as he made his way toward Ashton's favorite sailboat.

"I have work to do, Dad. I don't have time right now."

"Didn't you just tell Savvy … I like that name, by the way, very fitting," Joseph said. "Sorry. I got off track. But didn't you just tell Savvy that there's no use in arguing? Why in the world would you argue?"

Ashton blew out a breath and rolled his eyes before deciding to follow them all. "Fine. But we can't be out long," he said with a heavy sigh.

Savannah was in shock that he'd caved in so easily. He didn't seem to be the type of guy to be pushed around. Then again, when faced with three giants, he was probably wise to just go ahead and do exactly what they wanted.

"I love it when they behave," Richard whispered in Savannah's ear. "Don't you?"

She blushed another time and decided that dishonesty was the best policy. These men were way too overwhelming for a mild-mannered woman like her, so she didn't reply.

They boarded the most beautiful sailboat Savannah had ever stepped on. She was growing more uncomfortable by the minute, but she was stuck on this journey for now, so there was no use in being negative.

Before long, they set sail to a nearby island, and Savannah kept to herself in the back of the ship while the men raised sails and helped Ashton get the boat from point A to point B and so on. She would have loved to help them, but either she, or all of them, would probably have ended up taking an unexpected dive into the water.

She cursed her klutziness. It truly was a curse.

Just as she was really beginning to enjoy their journey, Ashton slowed the boat and then they were pulling up to a dock. The restaurant wasn't far away at all, so they strolled over to it.

They got a table without any delay. As she sat down with the powerful Anderson and Storm men, she couldn't help but think that she wasn't worthy of being there with them. Her family was nothing like these men, nothing at all. If they knew the whole truth about her, she doubted they'd be so eager to take her to lunch. She'd come up from a poor, abusive family. Her present company knew nothing of that kind of life.

But someday soon Savannah was determined to change her circumstances. She was going to have a doctorate, be a college professor doing a job she loved. She'd be making great money — relatively speaking, of course — and she'd get to play on the sea while doing research during the summers. Life didn't get much better than that. Her poor, miserable roots could be left behind, where they belonged.

"Are you enjoying working for Storm Adventures?" Richard asked her. "Apart from the fact that my son is forcing you to slave away under the hot sun."

Ashton said nothing as a waiter came and took their order for drinks. All the men were having a glass of wine, and she was thirsting for one, but unsure if she should go for the gusto. After all, she was the only one in the group who was technically still on the clock.

"Have a glass of wine, Savvy. One glass isn't going to make you inebriated or render you unable to do your job," Ashton said when she looked in his direction.

It was a bit creepy that he'd been able to read her thoughts.

So when she ordered and the glass arrived, she picked it up and took a sip. It was delicious. But she most certainly would need to pace herself.

"I love my job," she told the men, and she concocted yet another bold lie in hopes they'd drop the subject. "I honestly like working in the sun. I'm so pale, it's good to get some color." In truth, her pale skin was turning red no matter how much sunscreen she applied, but she was only going to say positive things about her job. She was sick of getting *the look* from Ashton.

Joseph snorted. "Red, except in wine, isn't a great color when you're burning at night," he said. "I don't think anyone truly enjoys baking all day long."

"I really do like it," she lied again.

"What other jobs do you have planned for Savvy?" George said to his nephew. "Your father already told you that she's far too qualified for only grunt work."

"What I do with my employees is none of any of your business," Ashton told them. "I don't appreciate the interference, and I haven't had any complaints so far. I treat my people well and pay them good wages. I'm providing free housing for Savvy, so I'd *think* she wouldn't have anything to be ungrateful about."

"I don't," she said quickly before this heated up any further.

"Humph. I think most of those tasks could be done by some of the young men you have running around out there," Joseph said.

"And what would *you* have Savvy doing?" Ashton asked.

Before the men could answer, the waiter came again and took their orders. It was a tough choice, but Savannah decided on a Caesar salad and Cast Iron Scallops. Yum. She was used to scarfing down cold turkey sandwiches for lunch, *processed* turkey, and this was a real treat. But the rich food was bound to make her sluggish. She'd try not to eat it all.

When the waiter left, the four of them began speaking again.

"I don't know. It's not my company, as you so kindly pointed out," Richard said.

Savannah did very little of the talking as the conversation continued. And though the men seemed to be bickering, with barbs flying back and forth, she did notice that there was a lot of love between them all, too.

She found it all highly entertaining — especially when the topic of conversation turned away from her. Soon, the food was there, yet the talking barely slowed. And before she knew it, her meal and wine were all gone, and her stomach was more than full. Yep, the rest of the day was going to be an ordeal.

And it was, because by the time they were back at the docks, Ashton's mood had never improved. Although Savvy didn't consider herself a violent person, she was thinking about making an exception to her rule.

CHAPTER NINE

THANK GOODNESS IT was almost quitting time, because this day couldn't get any more bizarre if a snowman came waddling down the pier and slapped her on the ass. Okay, that might be weirder than the day Savannah had had so far, but just a little bit.

Three days had passed since her impromptu lunch with Ashton, and she'd begun to notice a pattern. A *Twilight Zone* pattern that she wanted nothing to do with. One day the man was almost … dammit, the only word she could come up with was *sweet*. But then the next, he was the asshole boss from hell.

She never knew which side of the coin was going to land when he moved toward her. But there was only one more workday left in the week, and then finally she was going to get to see her sister. It was about time.

So she could put up with just about anything for another day. She looked down at her watch, noted the time, and made a slight amendment — another day and fifty-three minutes. No big deal.

But thirty minutes later, when she was putting away the cleaning supplies, she felt a sudden chill, and it had nothing to do with the breeze blowing in off the ocean. Savvy had no doubt that Ashton was standing within a couple of feet of her.

Dang it! Another fifteen minutes and she would have been safe and sound and inside hiding on her temporary boat. But of course Ashton knew her schedule. If he wanted to seek her out, he was going to do it, whether she was on the clock or not.

When she turned toward him, she almost drew back. Ashton normally wore shorts, polo shirts, or no shirt at all, and *Disarray* could have been one of his many middle names. The man ran his fingers through his lush head of hair more than any other person she knew.

Yes, she'd seen him in a suit once, when he was with his bimbo fiancée on the night of the show, but it had been dark and she'd had a buzz going on, so she hadn't gotten the full viewing pleasure. But right now, this man could be gracing the cover of *GQ* in a three-piece suit that made his shoulders appear a mile wide. Worse, his hair was brushed back, and his cheeks were tanned and firm. *So freaking unfair! Why didn't she have billionaire genes?*

She'd found him attractive before. Come on, she wasn't dead. But standing before her in all his glory, he was absolutely mouthwatering. That wasn't a thought she wanted to have about her bipolar boss.

"You're gaping at me, Savvy."

It took a moment for his words to penetrate her muddled brain. But with the accompanying arrogant smile now resting on his lips, his words computed and she grew instantly cranky.

"I'm most certainly not." Okay, maybe she could have come up with something a lot more biting than that. He'd caught her by surprise, though, and she was thinking ahead now for her next insult.

"Why lie?" he asked with a shrug. "You *obviously* like a man in a suit. Had I known, I might have worn one more often."

This time her mouth really was hitting the floor, but she managed to snap it shut. She didn't normally lack in intelligence, and it really bit her on the butt that she'd turned stupid in this man's presence. What in the world was wrong with her? She didn't like him, and besides that, she wasn't one of those girls who went all googly-eyed when they found a man attractive. Or at least she'd never been one of those girls.

"Is there something you wanted?" she asked at last when no stinging comebacks came to mind.

"Nope. I was just passing this way and thought I would say hi," he said after his eyes trailed from her head to her toes and then back up.

The pig didn't even try to hide his leering.

"Seriously, Ashton, are you this crude with every woman you're around?" she asked when he met her eyes again.

"Actually, no. I find you attractive. Why is that so offensive?"

"I consider it despicable that you not only find me attractive but that you harbor zero qualms about hiding it from anyone. In case you've forgotten, which is a distinct possibility, you have a fiancée," she said between clenched teeth. When was this man going to understand what that sentence meant?

"So what? We're not married yet, and I'm not dead," he told her with a shrug.

That jerk! He'd just used her unspoken line about not being dead. "You know what, Ashton? It's officially five o'clock, and I'm punching out," she told him as she turned away.

Before she got two steps he grabbed her arm and spun her around. His eyes narrowed and he pulled her in against his chest.

"One of these days, little missy, you won't be walking away," he told her.

Savannah didn't know how to reply to that. *To the moon, Ashton*? Definitely not.

His head bent forward just the slightest bit, and her body began to shake. That was certainly from fear and not desire. But before he did what she expected and kissed her, he let go and strode off.

It took several deep, cleansing breaths before Savvy could make her knees move again. How in the world could she feel even a lick of desire for that man? He was rude, crude, and a cheater. Why was her body so clueless?

"I don't know why you allow him to get to you like that."

One of her co-workers, Daisy, who couldn't be a week or two over eighteen, was sitting a few feet away on the dock with her feet dangling over the edge.

"You must have gotten a heck of a show," Savannah said with an embarrassed laugh. "And I don't know why I let him get to me. He just does." She sat down next to the nice young woman.

"The guy is pretty dreamy," Daisy said with a sigh. "If he wasn't so old, I'd totally have a crush," she added. "Well, I might have a crush anyway, but … gross."

"If only I thought he were gross, I wouldn't be fighting with myself so much," Savannah said, and she now chuckled openly. "It doesn't matter, though. The man is taken, whether he remembers that or not. And I'm not a cheater, not a homewrecker. So he can flirt all he wants, but I'm not doing anything with him. Besides, I'm only here for the summer and then I'll never see Ashton Storm again."

"I don't like his fiancée. She's never nice to any of us when she comes here. She actually told me to go up and wash her car once when she stopped in."

"Are you kidding me?" Savvy gasped. "What did you do?"

Daisy winked and gave a smile that would have done the Cheshire cat proud. "I washed it."

"Why the evil grin?" Savvy asked.

"'Cause I left fish guts in the rims. She complained for weeks to Ashton about her car being ruined because of coming down here. Finally some other workers washed it and they must have gotten those guts out. I don't think the people who washed it again cared for her any more than I did, 'cause they never told her."

"That's just terrible, Daisy," Savvy said, but her reprimand lacked a little force — she was laughing while saying it.

"The real plus is that she never asked me to wash her car again," Daisy told her before jumping to her feet. "I have to run. My boyfriend's going to be here any minute to pick me up."

Savvy sat out there a few more seconds and enjoyed the silence. Then she decided she'd best head in. The last thing she wanted was another run-in with Ashton. It was a wine kind of night — that was for dang sure.

CHAPTER TEN

What on earth was he trying to prove now?

Ashton stumbled onto the boat where Savannah was staying. He knew he was a fool to burst in on her while she was sleeping, but he couldn't seem to stop himself.

The woman had been working for him for the past few weeks, and though he'd told himself to avoid her, it seemed that he kept forgetting that and finding excuses to seek her out as often as he could. But that made sense. He was her boss, and he had to make sure she was doing a good job, didn't he?

Of course, anyone could do the crap work he was assigning her, so there really was no reason in checking in on her, but still … He knew it was petty of him to land her with tasks like that, but he was angry. She'd made him look at himself in the mirror, and he definitely didn't like what he was seeing.

He ought to ditch the fiancée, but, dammit, she was the wife he was supposed to have. So why in the fricking world was he seeking Savvy out?

Because when he tried backing off, he turned into even more of a jerkwad than he normally was. And his siblings and cousins had taken great pleasure in rubbing that pathetic fact in his face.

Okay, he was drunk yet again, and it seemed a perfect time to confront the far too sexy Savannah Mills. He knew, at least logically, that this wasn't likely to go well, but screw logic. It hadn't been his strong suit of late.

When he thrust open the door to her bedroom, he intended to shout, intended to wake her up and demand that she explain herself. Explain what, he didn't exactly know. She hadn't made a single move toward him — but, dammitall, he wanted her to. Maybe she could explain to him how she managed to have such control — over herself, and especially over him.

The moon was full in the sky and her curtains were open, casting a soft light in the room, offering him glimpses of her peaceful, contented expression as she lay there. Nice view, though most of her was under the covers. He was glad she wasn't on the lower deck, where he wouldn't have been able to see her face.

He swallowed what he'd been about to say. How could he wake her when she looked like a sleeping angel? He froze in the doorway when she twisted, kicking off the blankets from her long, smooth legs, giving him an excellent glimpse of her thighs, and making his trousers instantly tighten. *He* wasn't reacting at all like an angel at this moment.

Ashton was inside her bedroom now, and that was insanity. What he had to do was turn around and leave. But for some reason the command that he'd issued to his legs — *retreat* — wasn't registering in his hopeless brain. So now what? He didn't know. But he found himself moving toward her bed, sitting down on the edge … and then he was reaching out and brushing a strand of hair from her high cheekbone.

Suddenly the alcohol kicked in and his head was spinning. Falling backward, he nearly blacked out. When he reopened his eyes, he was grateful when he discovered his head next to Savvy's instead of against the hard floor.

He needed to move. Ashton knew that. He was lucky he hadn't woken her up with his tumble, but if she did wake and find him lying next to her, she was going to kill him — and rightfully so.

If his brothers could see him now, they would smack him upside the head. Okay, he'd get up in just a moment. Just as soon as the spinning came to a full stop. He closed his eyes and felt himself nodding off, but he fought it.

When Savvy shifted, her soft, sleek waist brushed against his arm, and the pulsing that it engendered down below took him to whole new levels of pain. This would certainly be the time to get up and leave. Pronto.

Damn. He was attempting to do just that when she turned and flung her arm across him. And the sexiest sigh he'd ever heard in his life escaped her sweet lips.

He was trapped.

Of course Ashton knew he wasn't trapped, but the feel of her warm breath against his neck, the touch of her fingers resting against his ribs — it was all too much to walk away from.

He wasn't normally a man who enjoyed intimacy. Sure, he loved sex. What red-blooded male didn't? But all the cuddle stuff, the quiet words at midnight, the talking of dreams and desires? Nah. None of that had ever appealed to him.

And yet, as he grew more and more sleepy while snuggled up close to Savvy, he thought that it was something he could get used to. This was the sort of woman who forever changed a man.

But he didn't want to be freaking changed. He was perfectly happy with who he was, and with the goals he had for himself in life. He loved his business, one that he'd grown exponentially, and he loved his fiancée. Okay, maybe he didn't love her, but he wanted to marry her. He did! She gave him good business connections through her well-established family. She made excellent arm candy. And she would produce perfect little Storm heirs.

Still, he couldn't shake how good it felt to have Savvy's arm resting across his tense abs, the smell of her sweet scent filling his nostrils, and the sound of her breathing lulling him into sleep.

Ugh! He couldn't think when he was drunk, especially when there was a sweet-smelling, softly sighing, achingly beautiful woman pressed against his side.

But even as he fought his desire, he knew it would be a losing battle. Maybe he just needed to bed her, get her out of his system, and then things would go back to normal. After all, he wasn't married yet. It was better to get this out of his system before he had a ring on his finger. That didn't make him a cheater. It made him a man sowing his final crop of wild oats.

That wasn't going to happen tonight, however. So he was going to leave — in just another minute.

But he had to keep his eyes shut for just a few moments. The day had been long and he was tired. He could blame it on too much sun, too much manual labor, and too much drinking. But the reality was that lying there with Savvy, her breathing soothing him into peacefulness, he just … he just …

He fell asleep. And then, when his guard was down, he pulled her tightly against him.

CHAPTER ELEVEN

A PIERCING SCREAM RIGHT in his ear shot Ashton instantly awake. Good thing he didn't need agonizing moments to brush the sleep off. He was either awake or asleep, with no in-between. Even with the impending hangover.

He flipped on Savvy's bedside lamp and then gazed at her. Although her hair was sticking out at odd angles, the woman was far too attractive. Okay, stunning. But he knew better than to voice his opinion right now as she clutched desperately at her covers and stared at him with gigantic pupils.

He'd expected anger, outrage, wild punches, and even murder from her if she found him in her bed. And he was certainly getting some of that. But as Ashton looked a little longer into her eyes, he saw something else, something that had his blood rushing through him in a hot flow of excitement. Sure, she was obviously horrified to find herself sharing a bed with someone she hadn't invited into it, but he couldn't miss the hint of arousal in her expressive eyes.

Interesting.

"I wanted to talk last night. I didn't mean to stay, but I … um … drank a bit too much and then somehow found myself right here," he told her. That sounded pretty good, didn't it?

"You shouldn't be in here, Ashton," she squeaked, looking down at his exposed chest.

When had his shirt come off? He didn't remember removing any of his clothes. Reaching below the covers he'd somehow managed to get beneath, he felt for his pants and was relieved when he found them still in place and still zipped up. He'd probably never know how the shirt had disappeared. But the appreciative light in her eyes while looking at his pecs made him glad it had.

"I know I shouldn't," he said. "But …"

"So *go*," she told him as if speaking to a child.

"One problem — I really don't want to."

She gasped and looked back into his eyes, but the look she was giving him suggested she was trying to figure out how many heads he had. Her attraction to him had gone south, and that wasn't exactly what he wanted from a woman he was sharing a bed with — well, unless *south* meant the region of his body getting harder by the second.

"I don't care if you want to or not," she said, her eyes narrowing dangerously. "This is my bed and I want you out of it. Now."

"Technically, doll, it's my bed."

She opened her mouth and gaped at him like a fish out of water. Or even a fish *in* water — a hungry fish? A fish who was really hungry but didn't want to admit it? Damn. He had to stop thinking like this. She'd be after his balls soon, and not in a good way.

"Really, Ashton? So you can just show up any time you please?"

"No. I probably shouldn't have climbed into bed with you, but now that I'm here, I have to admit that it's quite cozy and warm, and it smells great," he said with an exaggerated leer. He must have spent years practicing his eyebrow waggles.

Ashton hadn't planned to have feelings for this woman — feelings other than basic down-and-dirty lust — but as he sat beside her, enjoying the pink in her cheeks, the moistness of her lips, and the fire sparking from her eyes, he was enjoying himself immensely, and he actually liked her.

That was unexpected.

He wouldn't mind waking up like this every single morning.

Oh, sh … oot. That thought terrified him. Maybe it really was time to go. So why wasn't he moving? Hmmmm.

"I think your fiancée would be quite upset about this," Savvy said primly. "Or maybe the two of you have an open relationship. I assure you, however, that I want no part of something as sickening as that."

Scooting just a bit closer so his leg brushed hers, Ashton decided shocking and outraging this woman could become a favorite pastime.

"I'm going to break up with Kalli." That hadn't been at all what he'd meant to say. That hadn't been his grand plan. And he needed the trophy wife, so he opened his mouth to correct himself, but the words wouldn't come out.

"That's contemptible, Ashton. Let me understand this. You haven't even ended things, let alone taken any time to let your sheets cool off before you leap into bed with someone else. Do you think you're so appealing that I'll jump for joy and then jump you?"

"Well, kind of, yeah," he said. Maybe that wasn't so smart. Her eyes were blazing. Damn, if she were a comic-book superhero, he'd be fried right now. No comedy in that.

"No way that's happening. I can guarantee it. And I feel sorry for this woman."

"Why? The engagement is nothing more than a convenience for both of us." Ashton really wanted to tell himself to shut up. But that only seemed to be happening when he didn't want it to happen.

"How can you be so casual about breaking someone's heart? Are you that cold?"

"Breaking her heart? Did you not meet Kalli?"

"She obviously loves you, Ashton. You're engaged."

"You think love has anything to do with it? Don't you remember that old Tina Turner song? That's really precious. You are so naïve when it comes to the ways of the real world."

"You sound a little cynical."

"I'm a lot cynical, Savvy."

"But ... but the only reason to marry is love," she insisted.

"There's companionship, financial security, arm candy," he told her, which made her cute little lips part again.

"That's awful, Ashton. How can you say such horrible things?"

"What? I'm just speaking the truth. Would you date a man who can't give you security?" he asked.

He scooted down on the bed, tugging her down too before she was able to stop him, and then he lay there with his face only inches from hers. Her breath caught as he began caressing her arm.

"Yes, I would, Ashton. A man's net worth would have nothing to do with whether I was with him or not. I would only date a man if I had feelings for him and if he had the same feelings for me."

"Gotcha," he said with a wicked grin.

"What do you mean by that?" A shudder racked her enticing body.

"You have feelings for me," he told her.

"I do not," she spluttered. "And this is hardly a date, unless you want to call it a date which will live in infamy."

"I'm that memorable, am I? I can't claim to be one of the greatest generation, but I can be the greatest. Want me to prove that?"

"This is getting worse and worse."

"Are you going to lie to me, Savvy, and tell me you feel nothing when I brush my fingers against your skin?"

"Where do you get your dialogue? From cheesy romances?" she snapped. "Anyway, that's hormones, Ashton. Nothing more."

"And many a good relationship has started and endured because of hormones, Savvy."

"That's not the type of relationship I want," she informed him sternly.

"Liar."

"I'm not lying," she replied. "I don't do relationships based on sex."

"So you've never had sex?"

"I didn't say that!" She sounded very frustrated.

"So you've had lots of sex?" Why he kept pushing her buttons, he didn't know.

"That's really none of your business, Ashton, and even if I cared to share that kind of information with you, I certainly wouldn't do it … especially not *here*."

"Why not? I consider the bed a perfect place to share all our sexual secrets," he said, his body hardening more and more as he continued to caress her arm, his fingers getting perilously close to the swell of her breast.

"And I already told you that I have no desire to say anything about any sexual activities in my past."

"So you've had a lot," he said.

Surprisingly, he wasn't too happy about this, which made zero sense. What did he care how many partners she'd been with? He'd had more than his share, and no one was judging him — not that he knew of, at least.

"I'll say this one last time. I'm not speaking to you about who I have or have not slept with."

He couldn't read her, and that was strange. He could normally read everyone.

"Interesting," he said. No, it was hardly an original thing to say. But he had to fight to keep his tone even when he suddenly started imagining another man touching her body, making her cry out in ecstasy.

"This conversation has beyond gone in a direction I don't want it to," she told him, "and I'd like it to stop."

He tugged her against him and sighed with pleasure. Her breasts were finally pressed against him and he couldn't help but enjoy it as her nipples jutted out against his naked chest. Yup. She was definitely turned on.

"There's no stopping now," he said.

"Oh. So you're one of those guys who thinks 'no' means 'yes.' Just a prince of a guy. In any case, I need to use the restroom. I'd appreciate it if you left *now*."

Dammit! Now he had to stop. Because, no, he wasn't that guy.

With a reluctant sigh, he rose from the bed, but he turned toward her so she had no choice but to notice the bulge in his pants, the bulge she'd caused. Okay, so he'd had a part in that too.

"I'll give you your privacy, Savvy," he said. "For now," he added before swaggering to the door and making his exit.

Leaning against the wall right outside, he took a deep breath and tried to remind himself that he was only playing with this woman. He didn't want long-term commitments, at least not with her.

If he wasn't going to get sex from her, then there was no more use in pursuing her, right? Right! That meant this game was over.

Damn right it was over. He was going to go back to the fiancée who was perfect for him. That would be the smart thing to do. So that's what he would do. If only he actually believed it himself.

CHAPTER TWELVE

S AVANNAH TOOK A shower and brushed her teeth, which was no easy feat, because her body was a boatload of nerves. What had been going on just a few short minutes ago? Why had Ashton been in her bed? And why hadn't she tried harder to kick him out of it?

But it was time to stop daydreaming. Heck, where had her vocabulary gone? This had nothing to do with daydreaming — it had to be called *nightmaring*. Anyway, she had things to do, and now that it was Saturday, she had some time to do it. Throwing off the towel, Savannah pulled on her favorite skirt and then turned to grab her bra. Then she froze.

She'd been so preoccupied with her thoughts that she hadn't heard her door open. But open it was, and, blocking any view of the hallway, Ashton stood there holding a tray with muffins and coffee. It took a moment for her to raise her hands and cover her breasts. She was too stunned to react quickly. He stepped forward and she stumbled backward.

"Is breaking into my room something I can expect regularly?" she asked, mortification almost choking her. Sure, he'd been in her bed less than an hour ago, but at least then she'd had clothes on.

"I thought I'd bring you coffee and food. You were kind enough not to bellow too much at me when we had that little misunderstanding in your bed," he said before his eyes raked downward. Could he see right through her hands? She tightened her grip.

Savannah wasn't ashamed of her body, but she wasn't in love with it either. She could do a few more crunches, or tone up her arms more. She didn't want to get into her thoughts on her thighs, but they were covered, thankfully.

"Want me to look away while you finish dressing?" he asked.

His tone was a bit hoarse, and she didn't know what to say. Her words seemed to be locked deep down in her throat — not great if you wanted to win friends and influence people. He'd doubtless seen his share of naked women before. She just hadn't planned on being one among the masses.

"You can *leave*," she finally told him in yet another unnaturally high-pitched voice.

He didn't. He set the tray on the bedside table and turned to face the door. Not wanting to argue while she felt so vulnerable, she grabbed her shirt, threw it on, and did the buttons up crookedly. The bra would come later.

When Ashton looked back toward her, she was at least clothed, though she still felt incredibly exposed. She knew that he had a visual of her in his sicko mind, and that was a privilege she preferred to keep to her bathroom mirror.

He prowled up to her, and Savannah struggled again to find her voice as he brushed against her.

"I should have knocked. I'm sorry." He was whispering, but the sound — the vibrations — traveled all through her.

"Don't touch me, Ashton," she said.

But her traitorous body wanted to lean into the warmth she felt radiating from every part of him. Not good at all.

"I'll stop if you really want me to," he said. "Do we need one of those safe words?"

Safe word? What was that? But apparently all she had to do was tell him once again to get his hands off her, and he would do it, so why in damnation wasn't she opening her mouth?

Ashton's fingers crept up the sides of her neck and then he was undoing the tie holding her hair up, and soon her tresses were cascading past her shoulders and then he was gripping the back of her head and tugging her closer to him.

A mixture of confusion and desire rushed through her, and she knew she needed to call an immediate halt, but she just couldn't figure out why that was.

"Your body is stunning, Savvy. I want to see it again," he whispered, his words mesmerizing her. "I'm going to undo your shirt now."

She stood there silent as the first button came free. Her body shook with passion, passion she'd felt for only this one man. Then the first half of her shirt was open and his hand was sliding inside, his fingers coming closer and closer to her peaked nipples.

Enough. If she didn't end this right now, things were going to go too far, and she didn't want to live with the inevitable regrets. But as his fingers slid lightly over those nipples of hers, the only sound coming from her throat was a moan of pleasure.

Then he was gripping both breasts and squeezing the tender flesh, making her knees wobble. She had to grip his waist to keep from falling to the ground in a puddle. Yeah, right at his feet.

He pushed against her hips and she sighed again when his proud arousal made contact with her stomach. Okay, so he wasn't quite hitting the spot, the place lower down where she was pulsing with need. This should stop, but she hoped it wouldn't. She didn't want to want this so badly. But she couldn't help herself. No man had ever rendered her quite so speechless before.

"I'm so turned on, Savvy. I can't remember wanting a woman as much as I want you. I want to taste you, touch you, explore every inch of your delectable body. Tell me you want the same thing."

She couldn't fight this, couldn't stop what she was feeling. She wanted him, needed him, but there was no way she was voicing that thought aloud.

Savannah had been on some good dates before, but she'd never once felt the same desire for any of those men — or, to be more accurate, boys — that she felt for Ashton right now. Man, was she scared.

"Dammit, Savvy, tell me you like this," he commanded.

She only groaned. She couldn't say the words that he was trying to coax from her. It was taboo, against almost every principle she held dear.

He let out a similar groan of frustration and pushed her backward. Her knees hit the back of the bed and then she was tumbling on top of her mattress. She wasn't alone there for long. He dropped down with her, and before she could utter a word, his head lowered and his mouth replaced his hands as he sucked her nipple into his hot mouth.

While making her squirm beneath him, he rotated back and forth from one breast to the other while his hand found the edge of her skirt and began inching it up her thigh.

Seeing Ashton's dark hair on top of her fair skin was the most erotic image she'd ever witnessed in her life. It was all too much. Throwing her head back, she closed her eyes and gloried in the pleasure he was giving her.

Maybe it was knowing that this was wrong, forbidden fruit and tasty as sin, or maybe it was because she'd never done something like this before. But whatever it was, it was incredible, and she allowed her secret desires to be fulfilled as this hunk of a man licked and suckled at her breasts.

"I want to taste more of you," he growled.

A shiver traveled through her and all she wanted to do was scream *yes* in every language known to man. She wouldn't stop this now. She couldn't.

"Savannah!"

That didn't mean outside forces weren't a factor.

It took several moments for Savannah to realize that someone who wasn't Ashton was calling her name, and when she did, she immediately heard the footsteps drawing closer and closer to her door. Oh my gosh! The door was still open.

Thankfully, Ashton was aware of the situation, too, and though his eyes were burning embers of desire, he jumped back, tugging her skirt down and standing to block the view of whoever was about to step through while Savannah scrambled to button her blouse.

"Savannah, oh …"

Her sister had arrived.

In this sad hormonal meltdown, Savannah had completely forgotten about it. Alexa stood there for a moment before a big grin overtook her features, and she looked from Savannah to Ashton and then back. The man had so much gall that he didn't look embarrassed, not even a little bit.

"I'm, uh, I'm sorry," Alexa said, though she didn't appear to be sorry at all.

"No!" Savannah exclaimed before she forced herself to calm down. "I'm the one who's sorry, Lexie. I lost track of the time. Ashton here was kind enough to bring me some hot coffee, since he knew my pot broke last night," she said on the fly. The coffee pot really had broken.

Walking over to the tray, Savvy picked up the cup and took a big sip, though the liquid was now disgustingly cold. There was no way, though, that she was letting her sister know that, so she drank away.

"Oh, okay," Alexa said with the same stupid grin on her face. "If we need to reschedule, that's okay."

"No! I'm almost ready. Just give me a couple of minutes," Savannah said in a rush.

"Sure. Take your time. I'm going to soak up a few rays." Alexa turned and gave Ashton a quick once-over, which he seemed to enjoy.

"I'm Ashton, by the way," he said as he stepped closer to her sister.

Alexa gave Savvy a look that she didn't like at all before flashing Ashton a brilliant smile.

"I'm Alexa, Savs's younger sister," she said.

"Ah, the infamous sister everyone loves," Ashton said.

When he and her sister clasped hands, Savvy couldn't help but feel a surge of jealousy. Alexa was truly easy to love, and Savvy could see Ashton losing interest in her for her sister really fast.

But that wouldn't be a bad thing, because Savvy didn't want Ashton. She didn't, she argued with herself, even though it was ridiculous.

"I don't know about infamous, but I'm pretty great," Alexa said with a wink at Ashton before turning back to Savvy. "I'll see you in a few."

The look promised Savvy that she'd have to explain a few things. But still, Savvy breathed a sigh of relief when Alexa finally scooted away. Savannah was mortified at what her sister had to be thinking. With as much composure as she could muster, she turned to face Ashton.

"That won't happen again," she told him. This was composure? She was close to tears. "Now leave. I believe I said something like that before."

Ashton didn't say a word; he just took a step back and leaned against the wall. She had no idea what was in the man's head. What she did know was that she probably wouldn't like it.

Gathering up the rest of her clothes, she rushed to the bathroom. When she exited it, he was gone. If the fates were with her, Alexa wouldn't say a word about what she'd walked in on.

But when were the fates ever on Savannah's side?

CHAPTER THIRTEEN

"WELL, HELLO, LADIES."

Savannah and Alexa stopped in their tracks as a gorgeous six-foot-plus mountain of a man with a few days' growth of beard and piercing gray eyes stood in their path.

"Hello, handsome," Alexa said with a flirty smile before Savvy was able to even open her mouth.

"I'm Lance," he said, holding out his hand.

"I'm Lexie, and this is Savs. Nice to meet you."

But the moment Lance and Alexa's hands touched, Savvy was surprised to see her sister's eyes narrow a tiny bit and her smile fall away. Lexie tugged on her hand and Lance released it.

"Savs," the man said with a nod as he turned toward her. His smile was now just a little less bright.

"We have to get going now," Savvy said.

"Wait!" he called out as they took a step past him. They wheeled around. "Do you work here?"

This time Alexa was strangely quiet.

"I do," Savvy said.

"Good, then I know where to find you."

And then they walked around him.

"Maybe we don't want to be found," Alexa muttered.

"What was that about?" Savvy asked. "You were all flirty and then you were cold as ice."

"I didn't like the feel of that guy," Alexa grumbled.

"Like, you got a creepy vibe, Lexie?" Savvy was now worried. She hadn't felt anything creepy about the man.

"No!" Alexa blurted out. But her voice calmed. "Nothing like that. I ... I can't explain it," she said with something that sounded like frustration.

They walked on silently for a few moments and then Alexa's shoulders straightened and she seemed to be getting her groove back. Her eyes fixed on Savvy with a gleam in them.

"Spill your guts."

Ugh! Sisters! Even though they were through the gate and walking away from the docks, Savannah still turned around with a blush on her cheeks. She'd rather focus on the stranger and her sister's reaction to him.

"There's no way you're going to just pretend you saw nothing and drop this, is there?"

"Not a chance, sis," Alexa replied. "I can't believe that you've been getting down and dirty with that hunk of a man and you haven't mentioned it to me yet." She opened her car door and climbed inside. She was completely back to herself now. Maybe "Out of sight, out of mind" was her motto.

Savannah followed her reluctantly inside the small two-door and buckled up. This wasn't a conversation she wanted to have. What in the world was she expected to say to her little sis?

"That was the first and last time I'll be so-called getting down and dirty with him," Savannah said. "He's my boss."

"So what? I can't comprehend the idea of online dating. So where else are you supposed to meet people besides work, school, or the bars? And, seriously, the ones you meet at the bars aren't the ones you want to take home," Alexa said. "And I despise on-line dating."

"That's why I don't generally hang out at bars. But no, I don't want it to happen again with Ashton. That was a big mistake, and one I really, *really* don't want to discuss."

"Sorry, sweets. If you didn't want to discuss it, you shouldn't have been moaning in pleasure when I walked in," Alexa told her.

"I wasn't moaning in pleasure. I heard you calling me. We were just … well, he was kissing me," Savannah said. It was true, sort of.

"Hmm. Where exactly was the man kissing you?" Alexa asked.

Savannah's cheeks flamed again. Was her sister a freaking mind reader?

"None of that matters, Lexie. The man is taken. He has a fian-cée, so I shouldn't have been fooling around with him in the first place," Savannah had to admit.

For once her little sister was stunned into speechlessness, which made Savannah feel even worse about herself. Alexa was obviously judging her. She'd committed the ultimate of sins against her sex by poaching on another woman's territory. It was an unforgivable thing to do.

"Did you go after him?" Alexa finally asked.

"No. I've been trying to avoid him, but, as I told you, he's my boss, and so we keep running into each other, and then one mo-ment he's a complete ass, and then the next he's making me laugh …" Savannah trailed off when her sister chuckled.

"If you weren't chasing after some man, trying to steal him away, I don't see why in the hell you're feeling so guilty. You need to cut it out. Is this woman of his a saint, feeding the elderly every day, rescuing kittens from trees, saving the whales?"

"What in the world are you talking about?" Savannah sput-tered.

"If the guy is coming after you while he's already taken, it's for one of two reasons. He's either just a cad with zero morals," Alexa said, "or his fiancée is a class A bitch and he's looking for a reason to get away from her. He's heading for the hills, and your cute little hills are alive … never mind."

Savannah opened and closed her mouth helplessly as she tried to figure out how to respond to that.

"His fiancée isn't the nicest woman in the world, but that doesn't mean she should be cheated on, and it certainly doesn't mean I ever want to be the other woman."

"I agree. The guy needs to choose — either the fiancée or you," Alexa said simply.

"Not everything is always black and white, Lexie. It's not a bunch of true-or-false questions with easy answers."

"Sis, you have always sacrificed for others. Always. And I'm tired of watching you do that. Do you like this man?"

They pulled up at a shopping center, and Alexa cut the engine and turned to look Savvy in the face.

"No, not really," Savannah lied.

"I don't believe you. I think you do, or there's no way he would have been able to kiss you, let alone do whatever it was he was doing to make your cheeks glow the way they were when I walked into your room. I think you like him, but you are being self-sacrificing like always. If the man doesn't want to be with the fiancée, you have nothing to beat yourself up about."

"How can you be so casual about cheating, Lexie?"

"I'm not casual about cheating. I can't stand cheaters. And if the man were married, I would tell you to slap him in the face and run far and fast. But he isn't married, and it doesn't sound like he plans on getting married. So why not try to see if there is anything more to what's going on between you than insane lust?"

"Because I … well, I …" Savvy couldn't think of a single reason.

"Because you want to play the martyr. Well, stop it."

"I'm not playing the martyr, I swear," Savvy said. "I just don't like him, Lexie."

"Wrong. You do like him. Don't worry, though. I'll do some digging on him and find out if he's worthy of being liked or not. You don't always have the best judgment when it comes to men."

"It wasn't as if either of us had a great example of what a husband looks like," Savannah said.

"Yes, our father was an abusive asshole, and yes, I know you took the brunt of that," Alexa said before sending a warning look Savannah's way with one unmistakable meaning: DO NOT INTERRUPT. "Don't play it down. I've always known what you did for me. I also know that you're smarter than me and have always had bigger aspirations in life. We both got out of there, sis, and we won't repeat the pattern. We won't turn out like our mother, and we won't marry men like our father. So quit worrying so much about it and enjoy having a hot man drool over you. It's not wrong."

"I thought I hid a lot more from you than I apparently managed to do," Savannah said, stunned by this new confident woman her sister had become in the last year while working out of the country as a nurse.

"No. But I was selfish, and that's on my shoulders. I missed you so much while I've been gone. Phone calls haven't been enough. But now we're both in Seattle, and we're moving on with our lives. Let's do that without sacrificing anything else."

Savvy laughed. "Isn't it supposed to be me saying all of this to you?"

"You're only two years older than me, Savs, so loosen up a bit. You have two more months before your nose is stuck in the books again, and we're going to have a good summer. Hopefully, you'll also have some amazing sex with that hunk of a boss of yours."

"Seriously, who in the heck are you, Lexie?"

"I'm your favorite sister," Alexa said before opening her car door and jumping out.

Savvy followed suit. "Yes, you are," she said.

Lexie quit grilling her after that, and the two of them spent the rest of the day shopping, something Savvy detested. But they were also laughing, talking, and catching up on their lives.

By the end of the day, Savannah's worries over Ashton were nearly gone. Too bad they hadn't completely vanished, but she didn't want to get too greedy now, did she?

CHAPTER FOURTEEN

ASHTON SAT ON the deck of the boat and watched as Savvy walked away with her sister. His body was hurting, yet he was still smiling almost like a loon.

Never before had he woken up feeling so good. Hangover? What hangover? He'd never enjoyed his time with a woman so much, especially while not having sex. The conversation had been stimulating, intriguing. And it had left him wanting to keep it going.

The foreplay — well, that had been pretty freaking spectacular too.

And her words ... Oh, how those words had been a turn-on. She'd actually thought she would dodge him. It was a challenge, and the Storm men were known to love a challenge. His Anderson cousins apparently felt the same way, so it had to be in their genes. And maybe their jeans, too. Right down there.

Only moments after Savvy disappeared, Ashton watched as one of his brothers came strolling down the dock, a stupid grin on his face. Were stupid grins also in the family DNA?

"Damn, Ash, you have some mighty fine employees working here," Lance said as he jumped on board. "If I'd known that, I would have been coming around a lot more."

"You can keep your eyes *and* hands off my employees," Ashton said in his sternest voice.

"I can't help but look when they not only pass by me but also speak so damn sexily. They had legs that never seem to quit, plus the sweetest little asses — they were using their tushes to the best advantage as they positively sashayed along," he said with a sigh. "And why haven't you offered me a beer yet?"

"It's nine in the morning. You don't need a beer, Lance," Ashton told him.

"It's Saturday. There's no timeline on when you can pop the top. That dark-haired one had a great laugh." He was going to continue, but Ashton went on red alert.

"What do you mean? Did you talk to Savvy?"

"Savvy? You mean Savs? I think that's the name I was told. I'll definitely be visiting the docks a lot more often knowing that a babe like that is working here."

"Keep your hands off her, Lance." Bad move. His brother was already in goading mode, and the guy would show him no mercy now.

"Ah. I see you've also noticed the laugh." Lance moved to the on-deck fridge. He grabbed a nice cold one and sank into a deck chair as if he owned the world.

"No. She hasn't done much laughing around me," Ashton grumbled before his eyes lost their focus and he turned his lips up a bit. "But she can kiss. We're talking extraordinarily well!"

Lance wasn't above goading him again. "I thought you weren't supposed to kiss and tell."

"Some kisses are meant to be shared. No, not *that* way. Savannah is spoken for."

"Aren't *you* spoken for?" Lance asked casually. "I seem to remember some other woman …"

"Not for much longer," Ashton said. Maybe his trophy fiancée wasn't worth keeping after all.

"Message received," Lance said, taking a swig. "Didn't like Kalli anyway. But the sweet brown-haired sassy girl — Alexa was her name — I could find myself *really* liking her."

"Savvy's sister?" Ash said. Yeah, she was cute and all, but she didn't even come close to comparing to Savvy — at least not in Ashton's mind.

"Yeah. I'm definitely going to have to see what she's hiding beneath all that sass," he said.

"Go for it," Ashton told him. What color eyes did Savvy's sister have? He couldn't remember. He and his thoughts had been otherwise occupied.

Before Ashton said anymore on the subject, his brother was already moving on. "Why don't we now take it down a notch and get the sailboat ready to roll? I'm in need of some fishing."

"I thought Lucas was joining us," Ashton told him, and he stood up.

"He'll be here by the time we get everything ready. Since I have a feeling we won't be catching a heck of a lot of fish, we'd better bring a picnic basket. I'm already hungry."

"Screw that," Ashton said. "We'll just stop at Uncle Joseph's. You know he'll have a spread ready in minutes. He loves visitors."

"Yeah, I have a soft spot for the old man. I'm so glad Dad found his brothers, and even more glad the family was worthy of being found."

"Just a soft spot, Lance? I think you're going soft all over in your old age."

"As if you have a right to mock me, Ash. You don't feel the same?"

"Yeah, I do. I just don't admit all my girlie thoughts to the world at large," Ashton said with a laugh.

"Because I'm a nice guy, I won't mention the kissy-face stuff you subjected me to just now. And the family says I'm the one who needs to grow up," Lance said with a roll of his eyes.

"Ha! We both know that's so far from the truth, it's laughable. You're the most mature of all of us."

Lance gave out a booming guffaw. "I know. I just wanted to hear you say it."

"Yeah, that was *real* mature," Ashton said.

"Once in a while a guy has to let go. I've decided I've been too serious for too long. Where in the hell has that gotten me?"

"A successful business, for one," Ashton reminded him.

"Money only goes so far," Lance said.

Ashton's eyes flew open. "Are you telling me you're not happy?"

He stopped what he was doing and faced his brother. Yes, he and Lance joked around a lot, but they'd die for each another without even a moment's hesitation. They might have forgotten that for a short time, but their father had managed to bring them all back together, and Ashton, for one, was incredibly grateful.

"I'm happy … most of the time," Lance insisted, but his laugh rang false. "Okay, this is getting way too deep for a Saturday morning conversation. I just saw Lucas drive up. Let's get this show on the road."

Ashton wanted to push his brother, find out what was going on, but he also knew when to back off. If Lance wanted to tell him something, then he'd get around to it, but he would do it in his own time.

If a man needed his space, he had every right to it.

"Tell me more about this Savvy chick," Lance said. "I could see that she was curvy and hot with a beautiful smile and about the sexiest eyes known to woman. But does she have a brain cell alive?"

"What's that supposed to mean?"

"You tend to date — or in one notable case get engaged to — Barbie dolls, Ash."

"It's lovely to know you hold such a high opinion of me," Ashton almost snarled.

"Come on, brother. I'm already planning the party to celebrate your dumping Kalli. Not even Uncle Joseph, the man who thinks everyone over the age of eighteen should be planning marriage and grandbabies, likes that woman."

"I didn't notice," Ashton said.

He tried to remember family gatherings. And come to think of it, Kalli tended to avoid them. She'd always had one excuse or the other, but he hadn't cared enough to pay attention until Lance pointed it out.

"Yeah, Ash, and that's because you didn't look past the woman's pumped-up breasts to the beady look in her eyes."

"That's not fair. I saw her eyes plenty happy a few times."

"You sure about that?" Lance asked. "The woman can obviously act."

"You're in a mood today, big bro."

The two of them made their way down the docks to his favorite private boat. Ashton thought of it as small but he didn't do anything in small measures. This beauty was of the highest quality and was large enough for a couple of dozen people to fit on comfortably for an afternoon on the water, or else to house four couples for a week at a time. It boasted four bedrooms, two sitting areas, a large deck for sunbathing, spacious bathrooms, and an impressive modern kitchen.

He'd stayed on her for two weeks once with his brothers on a guys-only trip that had infuriated his sister, and they had seriously thought about sailing to Hawaii just to enjoy the peacefulness of the water while the rest of the world faded away.

Responsibility had called them back from that naughty jaunt, but that didn't mean he didn't go out on her as often as possible. Though he had a few dozen luxury boats, this one wasn't for charter. It was his personal baby, and he couldn't imagine ever finding a new favorite.

And just like that he'd somehow maneuvered his trail of reflections back to Kalli, as he realized the woman had never gone out on the water on his favorite boat. She hadn't liked any of the boats, and she'd told him more than once that she much preferred to keep her feet on solid ground. That should have been a huge red flag.

His head was about to explode now. Maybe he was blind, at least when it came to things he didn't give a damn about. And that was no way to be when thinking of spending the rest of his life with a woman.

"You guys aren't ready yet," Lucas said with an exaggerated sneer as he met them at the private boat.

"Ashton was otherwise engaged this morning," Lance said, and Ashton shot him a warning look. But Lance ignored it. "With his new employee."

"Oh, really?" Lucas said, and he was first in line to board the boat and move over to the controls. "I'm guessing this is a young, hot, well-endowed employee."

"Do you really think you're running the controls?" Ashton said as he pushed Lucas out of the way.

"A man has to try," Lucas said with a laugh.

"And don't talk about Savvy that way," Ashton added before he could stop himself.

Both Lucas and Lance stopped what they were doing and gave him looks he refused to let into his head.

"Let's just go," he said.

He heard Lucas ask Lance if the engagement to Kalli was off. He didn't stick around long enough to hear his brother answer. He had a boat to get ready to leave port. Besides, from what he'd just learned, he was sure to hear a happy whoop from Lucas, and that would be too much.

Ashton had been hoping for a relaxing afternoon. And while any time spent with his family was good, he also knew that he was going to be grilled. Or eaten alive. Hungry sharks roamed in these waters.

CHAPTER FIFTEEN

S AVVY WAS SAD to see the day end, but her little sister had to return to her apartment and get ready for her new nursing job. Savvy waved and didn't walk through the gates until her sister's taillights faded away. She'd see Lexie again soon — she was hardly about to let another year go by. Well, she wasn't going to unless her sister decided that her calling was again overseas.

She was proud of her sister, proud that Lexie used her talents to help those less fortunate, but that idealism had pulled the two of them so many miles apart before, and it could do so again. Neither of them was rich or likely to be, and international flights didn't come cheap.

When Savannah walked down the quiet docks, stepped onto her boat, and made her way to her bedroom, she wasn't expecting the impact of seeing the rumpled bedding, where she'd been writhing in shameless lust not too many hours earlier.

It stopped her cold, and the ache immediately started back up low in her belly. The way that man's mouth had caressed her body had been magical. She had a feeling she wasn't ever going to feel something so earth-shattering — or ocean-shattering — again.

No. She couldn't think like that. Though she might not be the most romantic woman in the world, she did believe in love and did believe that she wouldn't be alone forever. But she'd never settle with just any man, especially an engaged man, even if he couldn't seem to remember he was taken. Even if her sister told her it was all fine and dandy. She just didn't think that way.

Shaking off thoughts of Ashton, Savannah threw herself into cleaning mode, stripping her bed, washing the sheets, then cleaning up her room, trying to erase all scents of Ashton from it. It wasn't working. She could still smell the man even after the bedding came out of the dryer. By the time she was finished, the sun was low in the sky, promising a spectacular sunset. And there was nothing better than sitting on the deck and watching the colors paint the skies.

The moment she sat down, of course, thoughts of Ashton stroking her in all the right places flooded her mind, sending instant fingers of delight throughout her. Yes, images of his mouth on her nipples, his hand sliding up her inner thigh.

She shuddered and tried to catch her breath. If she had these thoughts too often, working for the man wouldn't work at all. And she wanted this job, wanted to be on the ocean, wanted to be right where she was.

"What are you doing sitting out here all alone?"

Startled by the deep baritone, Savannah froze. But when she turned, she found a smiling Richard Storm approaching her.

"I love sunsets, and I'm hoping for a good one tonight. This is the perfect view right here," she told him. "Would you like something to drink, or are you just passing by?"

"I would love a drink. But why don't you come with me to have it? I have a much better spot to watch a sunset from," he said, holding out his hand and looking at his watch. "I'd say we have about an hour to get situated before the colors begin."

"I don't know ..." Should she hang out with Richard when she thought the man's son was a cad? It didn't seem right.

"Aw, come on. I want to take a little ride, and it's lonely all by myself."

She chuckled. "If you put it that way, then I really don't have a choice, do I? Are we going to watch from deeper out to sea?" she asked as he urged her along to a smaller boat and helped her up.

"No. Just a better location."

She didn't think to question him further. But within a few minutes the boat was pulling away and they were racing along the water.

It was her first evening boat ride here in Seattle, and laughter spilled from her as the cool night air whipped through her hair. Seriously, there was no place she'd rather be.

Far too quickly, though, the boat slowed down, and Richard began moving toward a large lit-up dock. And then she saw a bright bonfire and a crowd of people in beach chairs sitting around it, and several other people moving across the sand-covered shoreline.

"What are we doing?"

"This is the spot to watch the sunset," Richard said as he cut the boat's motor.

"Is this your place?"

"It's my brother Joseph's house."

"I don't want to intrude," she told him.

"I guarantee you that Joseph will be upset if you don't join me, sweetheart."

Richard was genial about it, but what choice did she have? Leaving would be not only rude but also impossible. How was she to get a ride back?

Just as she was giving in, she spotted Ashton. She so wasn't ready to speak to her boss again, not after what had happened that morning. And not after the thoughts that her sister had placed in her head.

"Let me introduce you to some of the family," Richard said, pulling her attention from Ashton, who was laughing at something one of his friends or family members had just said to him.

Before Savvy knew what was happening, she was swarmed, and people were throwing names her way. There was no way she would remember all their names. But she really wouldn't have to anyway. It wasn't as if she'd be hanging around this wealthy crowd. She was only a worker, not on their social level at all.

Name after name, handshake after handshake continued her way. Lucas, Alex, Mark, Trenton, Crew. She finally gave up on even trying when the wives and children were all standing in front of her.

"Come sit down for a minute with us 'girls,'" one of the women said. "The Anderson and Storm men can be quite overwhelming."

Dammit! Savvy couldn't remember her name, but she wasn't about to ask her to repeat it.

The woman laughed. "I'm Brielle, married to Colt, that devastatingly handsome man over there by the fire with Ashton," she added.

He was pretty dang handsome, but Savvy hadn't noticed before now. It was hard for her to look beyond Ashton, even if she told herself to do it.

"I'm Cassie, Trenton's wife," a pretty blonde said. "I wish I weren't nursing — parties suck when you can't drink alcohol. Never mind me, Savvy, have an extra for me. Now give us the scoop on Ashton. We've heard rumors that the Wicked Witch of the West — or is she from the East? — is long gone." She grinned happily as she said that.

"If you ... um, mean his fiancée, I don't know. I believe they're still together," Savvy stammered.

"Oh, come on. He's been so different since a pretty brunette has been hired to work for him," another woman said.

Was it genetically impossible for one of the Andersons or their brides to be ugly? Savvy was beginning to think so. "I'm Kyla," the woman added as an afterthought.

"I just work for him," Savvy told the women, shifting on her feet as she looked down. She wasn't exactly lying. She did just work for him ... when she wasn't allowing him to strip off her shirt and run his tongue along her skin.

The mere thought brought a blush to her cheeks.

"Yeah, we heard Richard and his brothers set up the job interview," Amy Anderson said. Savvy recognized her.

"Yes, Richard was at a job fair at my school," Savvy told them, not thinking anything strange about it.

"That's how it all starts," Emily said. "I met Joseph that way, and he offered me a cooking job. I just didn't know it was for his amazingly hunky and very single son Mark," she said with a giggle. "But I am so grateful to the man because I love Mark and our children so much."

"Surely he wasn't trying to match you up," Savvy gasped.

"Of course he was. That's what the meddler does. Then his brother George moved home, and they did the same with his kids. Now, they've found Richard and the fun continues," Jessica said with her own laugh.

"That's not at all why Richard suggested the job," Savvy told them. There would be no way Richard could think she was good enough to marry his son.

"You can think that if it makes you feel better," Amy said, smiling. "But you'll go through a lot of heartache in the meantime."

"I'm not hurting," Savvy assured the group of women.

But all the women in the group wore a knowing smile that had her worried.

Still, she found that after a few minutes with them, her nerves were beginning to calm. This large, wealthy, famous family was acting like any other family she'd had the privilege of spending time around. And they were all welcoming her.

They were nothing like what she'd have thought. She was a bit jealous, in fact, to see that a family could live this way — full of love and laughter and gossip that wasn't meant to hurt anyone. What an incredible life they shared together.

The kids ran around together, collecting shells, dipping their feet in the water and roasting marshmallows at the fire while squealing in delight when one of their parents would chase them all down.

But the second Ash spotted her as the crowd parted, she watched as he made a beeline for them. She had no chance of escape unless she planned to dive into the ocean. And to judge from previous experience with the man, she had no doubt he'd dive in after her.

Her nerves took over, and she missed the last thing Amy said to her.

"Ah, Ash is on his way over," Emily said with a chuckle. "I was wondering how long it would take for him to figure out you were here, Savvy."

Richard reached them right before Ashton did.

"I'm sorry, darling. I got to visiting with my brother. Can I bring you anything?" he asked politely.

"I think a six-foot-plus hunk would cure her thirst," Jessica said beneath her breath, making Savvy's cheeks flood red.

Thank goodness it was dusk.

"Don't worry, Savvy. We've all been where you are right now. We'll give you some privacy," Amy told her.

And much to her horror, the women and kids slipped away, leaving her standing with only Richard, and Ashton just about there.

"I was hoping my father would bring you back here," Ashton said.

She couldn't read his expression. But maybe she didn't want to.

"I didn't know you were the one behind all this." She spoke in measured tones. She wanted to shower him with just enough disdain to show him what she thought of him and his tactics, but without seeming like a complete ... wench in front of his father.

"I wasn't exactly behind it," he told her. "I just mentioned to my father that you enjoyed sunsets."

"Well, I'm enjoying your father's company, so you're free to leave us now," she said through gritted teeth. She really hated being manipulated.

"Do you prefer older men now, Savvy?"

She gasped at the outrageous comment.

"I can't believe you would embarrass Savvy this way, Ashton," Richard told his son in the scolding tones of yesteryear.

"You're right, Father. I apologize," Ash said before giving her a once-over that had her on edge again. "You look very beautiful tonight, Savvy."

She tried to find the undertones in his compliment, but there weren't any that she could spot. "Thank you," she finally mumbled.

"I must say, though, that I preferred what you were wearing when we woke up."

Savvy's cheeks flamed painfully as she looked to the ground in utter mortification. How could Ashton say that in front of his father? Did he have zero respect for anyone? Richard must think she was a complete trollop now. And she liked the man — his opinion meant something to her.

"That fire over there looks like it needs some more fuel, Ash. Why don't you go add some, and maybe trip into it while there?" she told him so sweetly it took Ashton a moment to realize what she'd just said. But instead of the anger she'd hoped for, she saw his lips twitch upward.

"It looks like you don't need me here," Richard said with a twinkle in his eye, and then the man abandoned her. She decided that all the Storm men were traitors.

"Are you having a bad day, darling?" Ashton asked her. "You seem slightly hostile." Before she was able to stop him, he was winding his arm around her back. "Maybe I can make it better."

"I'm not your darling," she snapped. "Let go of me."

"But I like holding you. I can see it becoming an addiction."

"Oh, Ash! I forgot, but I promised Savvy a beautiful sunset," Richard called out from about twenty feet away. That loud announcement made several people turn in their direction, and Savannah wanted to find a hole, jump in, and let the sand bury her.

"Then that's what she'll get," Ashton called back. He finally took his arm off her back, but offered her no freedom. The arm went around her waist and tugged her to his side. "Let's go watch it. I have a perfect place in mind."

Savvy bit her tongue until they were out of hearing range of the crowd. Then she yanked against Ashton's determined hold on her. "What do you think you're doing?"

He wasn't letting go. That was for sure.

"It's a beautiful night. The sun is setting and I'm with a spectacular woman. Do I need to put a definition on what it is?"

"That's not what I mean. Why are you acting this way? Why are you mauling me? We aren't a couple, and I don't want your family to start thinking we are."

He led her up a small hill, where a private bench was set back from the beach, offering privacy while still giving a great view of the water and the colors splashing across the sky.

"Maybe I've decided I'd like for us to be a couple," he said, shocking her. He helped her to sit down — all this touching! — and sat right next to her.

"You have a fiancée," she growled.

"I'm rethinking that situation," he told her.

"But right now, right at *this* moment, you're engaged to be married. I'm no poacher." She was at her starchiest, and was sitting there stiffly beside him. "I'll add that even if you were single, I wouldn't accept a date with you after all your uncouth behavior."

"Aw, come on, Savvy, I was just poking some fun."

"I wasn't amused," she told him. "I'm still not."

"Then I'll just have to find other ways to enthrall you," he said.

What was the point of even talking? He wasn't listening. So she stayed silent for several heartbeats as the sun continued to set in the sky, but for once the colors weren't inspiring any peace inside her. She had to speak again.

"We have nothing in common, Ashton. Besides that, you *are* my boss, making this completely inappropriate. And, as if we need another reason not to date, I start back up at school in about two months. Even if you *were* going to be free, I'm not looking at getting into a relationship right now."

But his hand was resting on her thigh and damn if she didn't like having it there.

"Ah, Savvy, those are all just excuses and ways to hide from the world. If a person wants to be with somebody, he — or she — won't let anything get in the way."

"Maybe I want those things in my way, Mr. Storm." And maybe using his last name would send a clearer message.

"And sometimes these obstacles are what make us stronger, braver, and more able to see all possibilities."

"Ha. You're not looking for anything more than a good time in the sack." She wasn't born yesterday.

"You don't know what I'm looking for — unless you can suddenly read minds," he said.

Savannah reached for his hand, which was still on her thigh, and she dug her nails in. She had to drive him away — his touch was too confusing. But her tactic didn't work. He simply flipped his hand over and gripped her palm before lifting it to his lips and kissing it, sending tingles throughout her body.

"I know you once had a reputation for being a playboy, for changing women as often as you changed clothes. And that still seems to be the case, because you keep forgetting about the woman with your ring on her finger. I have no interest in being with a man who can dump his fiancée because he suddenly grows bored."

"Hmm. You've been checking up on me. I like that," he said, making her want to scream in frustration.

"Ugh. I'm trying to tell you that we would never be a good couple. We are much too different for that ever to happen!"

"I disagree, Savvy. As I've said before, I think we're surprisingly alike. But besides that, isn't the reason behind dating to get to know each other? Then if two people find they don't like what the other has to offer, they go their separate ways. My take? I have a feeling we're not going to find things about each other that we don't like."

How couldn't she be exasperated? "You don't know me!"

"I know what I want to know. You're smart and funny, a hard worker, and sexy as hell. Your smile is the brightest thing I've ever witnessed, and your touch — hmm, your touch takes my breath away."

"Ashton…," she began with a sigh and then stopped talking. She didn't know what to say next.

"Just admit that you liked what we did this morning, Savvy, and not just the touching. You enjoyed the talking as well. We click in a lot of ways. There's nothing wrong with liking each other or saying so out loud."

She didn't want this. She wanted to be mad, upset, disgusted. That protected her from the games he was obviously playing. She'd lived through enough misery in her youth, and as God was her witness, she'd never be vulnerable again.

"If I listen to what you have to say, will you leave me alone?" she asked with a huff.

"I might agree to that," he said.

"Fine. Then speak. I'm all ears," she told him, only a hint of sarcasm in her voice.

"Good, Savvy. I'm glad you're finally being reasonable."

Now, she was going to explode. "Reasonable? *Reasonable?* You are the most irrational and ill-bred ass I've ever met in my life, and that might be including my worthless father."

"You're so cute when you're mad, Savvy, doll. We had a good time this morning. I'm man enough to admit that I want you more than I want my next breath. We've already tested the water, so why not get to the finish line? We're both adults, consenting adults, and we're not hurting anyone by getting into a relationship."

"We're hurting your *fiancée*, Ashton." She kept herself from screaming, but just barely.

He brushed his hand in the air as if Kalli were no more than a gnat he was soon going to squash. If Savvy got into any sort of relationship with him, she would soon be the woman he was swatting away. No way! No how!

"It's over except for the Dear Jane letter, Savvy. You know that."

"I'm delighted, Ash. Forgive me for what I said before. You're clearly the soul of reason." Did she sound a bit ironic? " But I think I'll pass on the relationship."

"Why?" He looked confused, but men weren't known for reasoning ability.

"I've already told you why, but since you don't seem to be listening to me, something you're very versed in *not* doing, I'll add that as a *reason* as well. I would never enter into a relationship with someone who doesn't know how to listen to what I need and want — who doesn't actually hear a word I'm saying."

"I listen," he spluttered. "I just don't like what you've been saying so far."

"I'm not going to sleep with a man because I'm the most convenient person around for him to get his jollies off with. *Love the one you're with* and all that crap."

"You weren't protesting this morning, Savvy. You can't hide how you feel when we touch. And you were on fire."

"I believe in relationships, Ashton, not casual sex. I don't sleep with a man for the heck of it. I have to love him first." He could mock her all he wanted for having morals, but she wasn't going to allow him to make her feel bad about it.

"How can you fall in love if you don't have chemistry?" he challenged her.

"If you're in love, you *will* have chemistry," she shot back.

"It's a really lonely road, the one you're taking. You can have all the morals you want, but if you fight what you want, what you need, that doesn't make for good bedfellows. It doesn't keep you warm at night and it doesn't soothe the ache your body feels."

"I can soothe my own aches," she snapped.

When those words registered, her cheeks flamed absolute crimson. No, she hadn't bought a vibrator yet.

But he guffawed. "Trust me, doll. It's always much better to have someone else doing the soothing than to do it on your own."

"You know that wasn't what I meant. I just don't need another person in my life to make me feel okay about myself."

"That's good for you. But I'm not giving up. I won't force you, Savvy, but I have a feeling you'll come begging soon enough."

He leaned closer to her as he whispered these last words, the added darkening of the sky the perfect backdrop to this unreal night.

He leaned in to kiss her, and she suddenly got some of her brain cells to fire in the right direction. When she brought her hand up to deflect him in the nick of time, Ashton wasn't taken aback. He kissed her palm, which still felt good, but at least he didn't make contact with her lips.

This time when she tugged against him, he released her. Smart man. Her next gouge of the nails was going to end up in a place that he wouldn't like at all.

"I'm going now, Ashton. Maybe if you ever learn how to listen to what I'm actually saying, I will take seriously, or somewhat seriously, what you're spouting off. Until then, don't bother talking to me."

She began walking away, but he quickly followed her.

"Explain what that means," he demanded.

"It means that suave lines, threats, and facetious comments aren't the way to gain my respect. If you really want to get close to me, that's something pretty dang valuable to know."

She walked away again. This time he let her. It didn't take her long to find Richard, and thankfully, he was willing to give her a ride back to the docks. She'd had enough of Ashton Storm for one day.

CHAPTER SIXTEEN

THE WATER UNDERNEATH her boat had been lulling her into a sense of peace. But Savannah was now sitting up with her phone pressed against her ear and her spine ramrod straight.

"No way!"

"Don't be a wuss, sis," Alexa said. "You promised me, remember?"

"That doesn't mean that I've agreed to go out on random blind dates," Savvy told her.

"You don't need to yell. And I adore this man. I've known Darren for a year now and I showed him your pics and he was all over taking you out."

"If he's so great, why in the world aren't *you* going on a date with him?" Savvy asked.

"He's your type, not mine," Alexa said.

"What's that supposed to mean?"

"It's not an insult, Savs. He's just supersmart like you, but I promise he's also a total babe."

"I'm not doing this, Lex. Absolutely, positively, one hundred percent NO." Savvy needed to stay firm.

"Please, sis. If you don't go, he'll think I'm a big liar." Alexa was now using the voice she'd always used while they were growing up. That pathetic wheedling voice she used to get her way, with hints of impending tears. Fake tears.

Dammit! It was working. But Savvy had to fight this off.

"Last weekend, weren't you telling me that I needed to go for it with my boss?"

"Well, nothing is happening on that front," Alexa said, "and I don't want you to die an old maid."

"I'm only twenty-four, Lexie. And *old maid* is an outdated and hopelessly sexist term, useful now only if you're playing cards in a family setting."

"Would you prefer *spinster*? I know, I know. But it's just one date, Savs. If you hate it, you can yell at me for a full two hours tomorrow. Promise."

It was a Friday and Savvy was sick of sitting around and doing nothing in her little room. Maybe it wouldn't be so bad to go out with this guy. What was the worst that could happen? Okay, a lot of worse things could happen. But on a positive note, the night could be fun. And if not, she got a free meal, didn't she? That was always good on a tight budget.

"Fine. I'll go. Give me the place and time," Savvy said, and jotted the information down. At least the restaurant was in walking distance. "You owe me, Lex."

"I think you're going to be the one owing me after you meet this guy."

Savvy hung up the phone and got ready. Her pushy little sis had given her only two hours to make this date. But Lexie also knew Savvy well, and if she'd had too much time to think about this, she would surely have found a way to get out of it.

Dressed in a knee-length summer dress and flats — there was no way she was wearing heels — she threw her purse over her shoulder and made her way up the dock. Thankfully, she didn't run into her moody boss. Maybe her luck was turning around.

She arrived at the bistro in about ten minutes and then wasn't sure what she was supposed to do. Her sister really hadn't given her enough information. Was she supposed to go inside? Wait at the bar? Meet him out front? The guy knew what she looked like, but she had no clue what she was getting herself into. Maybe she should just hightail it out of there. So what if her sister looked bad? Savvy was preparing to make that quick exit.

"Savannah?"

Ooh, that voice had possibilities. Turning, she found a nice-looking man, *very* nice-looking man, walking up to her wearing a pale green button-up shirt, a pair of designer jeans, and Doc Martens. His hair was dark and short, and he had brilliant green eyes. Not bad at all.

"Yes. You must be Darren," she said.

"Yes. Darren Tessler. I have to say that your pictures don't do you justice."

Smooth. The man was smooth. But he wasn't dangerous — that was her next thought. Not dangerous like Ashton.

"Thank you. I would say the same, but my sister didn't give me a picture," she said with a laugh. "I don't normally do blind dates, but ..." There really was no but, *but* her nerves were making her begin to babble.

"Your sister has only great things to say about you. I feel as if I already know you," he said. "Shall we go inside?"

Shall we? Wow. Good-looking *and* manners to boot. So far, so good.

"I haven't eaten here yet, and I'm starving, so I hope it's good," Savannah said. When she realized her words, she blushed a little. Should she admit she was that hungry? Wasn't she supposed to order a salad on a first date? To hell with that. She never had been one of those size-zero types. She wasn't in any way heavy, but she just decided, most of the time at least, to embrace her curves.

"Nice. Me too — I mean that I'm also in that condition," he said as he opened the door for her. "I'm glad you aren't one of those girls — sorry, *women* — who come to a great bistro and then just order lettuce and no dressing."

No. That certainly wasn't her. Not unless there was a man near her who was making her stomach churn. A man like Ashton Storm. No way! She would not think of that man's name while she was on a date with another guy. It was rude and it was stupid.

They were shown to their table, a nice intimate seat in the back of the room with a low-hanging modern chandelier over the center. This Darren fellow had chosen well for a first date.

"Do you prefer red or white wine?" he asked as he looked at the drink menu.

"White please, and not too dry. I'll warn you now that I just drink the wine I like and don't worry about pairing it with my food." It was better to let him know at the outset that she wasn't a food snob. Kalli, she was certain, would be horrified by such a statement. Dang! She was getting far too near to Ashton territory again.

"Good, Savannah. I'm the same way."

Was he? She had no idea, but he earned a few more points in the good-guy column.

Once their order was placed, her date focused solely on her. It was a little overwhelming with those bright eyes of his, which seemed to have a permanent sparkle to them. How in the world was this man still single? And why didn't she feel a tightening in her stomach when he was sitting so close?

"How do you know my sister, Darren? Did you serve overseas with her?"

"No. I met her before she left for Africa, and we continued our friendship over email while she was away. I did get to go there about six months ago with a buddy of mine."

"Doing what?" she asked.

"I'm an architect. My friend develops affordable housing there, and I helped him do some builds on my time off. I enjoyed it the first time so much that I'm most likely going back each year."

Dang! This guy was a freaking saint. She reached out and touched his hand, wanting so much to feel a spark. Nothing …

What in the hell was the matter with her? She wasn't going to give up quite yet.

"Wow, that's an interesting job. Do you love it?" If she weren't so in love with the ocean, architecture would have been her career choice.

"Yes, I knew from the time I was a boy playing with Legos that I was going to create unique buildings. And the first time I saw a finished project of mine, I just stood in front of it in awe. I don't think I left for like six hours. I still occasionally stroll by that place. It's my favorite."

He was obviously proud of what he did, but he wasn't acting arrogant about it. The conversation enthralled her — it was no wonder her sister liked him so much — and before she knew it, she and Darren were laughing as they shared dessert.

All too soon it was time to leave. As he stood and helped her up, she once again thought approvingly of his manners. Then she was filled with more disappointment. His hand was resting on her lower back as they left the restaurant, and she still felt no hint of excitement.

Savanna decided right then and there that she must be suffering from a disorder of some sort. Seriously!

Darren insisted on walking her back to the docks, and Savannah secretly delighted in that. She liked a gentleman. Yes, much of the etiquette was silly, but gentlemanly behavior was something her father had never displayed in any way. So she liked having her chairs being held for her and her doors being opened. She especially liked a man who insisted that she make it to and inside her door safe and sound. Granted, she didn't have much of a door right now. She had a boat. A boat that didn't belong to her.

"I've had a nice evening, Savannah. I would love to see you again soon," he said as they stepped up to the boat.

Should she go out with him again? Did she even have time? But what would it hurt? She wasn't seeing anyone, unlike her snarky boss. She was free and young and still had about two months before school started, at which time dating would be a no-no.

"I'd like that," she heard herself saying.

Uh-oh.

And then Darren was moving closer to her and she knew he was about to kiss her. She wanted to back away, but that was stupid. There was nothing wrong with a kiss at the end of a nice date. This wasn't the 1950s.

And then the choice was taken from her. Darren's arms wound around her and his lips were on hers.

It was a pleasant kiss, not too aggressive, not too soft. Just … pleasant.

"Thank you again," he said before taking a step back.

"Thank *you*, Darren. I had a lovely time." And with that she walked onto her boat.

She knew that she felt no spark when she didn't even sneak a peek of him walking away. Darn it! Well, she was going to go out on another date with the man. Maybe the attraction would grow. Love at first sight was a myth.

Before she could get to her room, she heard her name spoken again. And this time the sound sent a shiver down her spine.

"Savvy, I need to speak with you."

The instant tingling that rose up in her stomach when Ashton's voice reached her ears filled her with fury. Maybe she was more like her mother than she'd ever wanted to be. Because she had to be crazy to feel anything toward this man, a man who was completely wrong for her.

She stepped reluctantly away from her room and went back out to the docks, where Ashton was waiting, a scowl on his face. Big surprise.

"What do you need, Ashton?" She stayed as far away from him as she could. He looked to be in a worse mood than usual.

"This is a secure dock, Savannah, and I don't appreciate seeing you bring anyone you please down on it."

It took a moment for Ashton's words to process, but when they did, she glared at him. All the employees brought people down onto the docks. She'd never heard of this rule before.

"I don't bring many people down here, Ashton. I've brought my sister and —"

Before she could finish, he cut her off. "And some strange man who could be scoping the place out."

"I did not. He was my date and he was walking me back to my place," she said through clenched teeth.

"I thought you didn't have time to date," he said, taking a menacing step toward her.

"My dating life is none of your damn business, Ashton. I'm not on the clock right now." She turned to leave.

"I'm not done speaking with you yet," he said.

Savvy whirled around and tapped her foot. When he didn't say anything right away, she let out a frustrated sigh.

"What do you want to say that doesn't have to do with my personal life, Ashton? I'd like to get to bed."

His eyes sparked at her mention of *bed*, and Savvy wanted to kick herself, and him too. But she just waited.

"One of the boats is leaving in one week for an Alaskan cruise. You need to train with Shirley to be ready for it. Starting Monday."

His mention of a cruise took her bad mood and tossed it in the gutters. And she gave him a genuine smile, the first that he'd brought to her lips in a long time.

"That's wonderful news. Thank you!"

"The ship will be gone for ten days. Are you sure you can handle being away for so long?" he said with a tinge of venom.

"Trust me, I could be away a month without a single problem if I were lucky enough to be on the ocean all that time," she replied. She decided not to respond to Ashton's bad temper.

"Fine. Be ready."

And he began to walk away. Savvy sighed and headed back to her boat. But she suddenly felt Ashton's hand on her arm and then she was being whirled around. She was exhaling frantically, too stunned to speak when he tugged her against him.

"This is a goodnight kiss," he said.

His lips connected with hers before she had even a tiny moment to try to protest. And while she could still think, her last thought was that he was right. This did count as a real goodnight kiss.

His mouth was masterful and commanding as he held her tightly pressed against his body. His lips eased hers open, and she didn't have a thought of fighting him. Her heart thundered as he controlled the kiss as if he'd been doing it forever.

The kiss could have lasted seconds or hours. But when he finally released her, she stood there in front of him wobbling on legs now made of jelly.

"That's better," he said. Then he walked away.

Savvy didn't move for several moments, too shocked to take a single step. Finally, she got her limbs to obey her and made her way onto her boat. She sat on her bed in a whirl of confusion.

She should have been outraged at what he'd done just then. But her excitement drowned that out. She was about to spend time on the ocean. Sure, it wasn't diving for treasures, but that would come soon, too. The point was that she was going out to sea.

Nothing could dampen her mood now. Not even alternately uptight and passionate bosses who made her stomach do flip-flops and who made her legs weak and her system shut down.

CHAPTER SEVENTEEN

THE WEEKEND'S DRAMA was over, such as it was. Shirley had taken charge, and Savannah had a uniform and was getting rather good at making hospital corners on the bedsheets and disinfecting the showers and the toilets. Talk about fun! At least she got to put chocolates in bowls and make animals out of towels.

Best of all, Ashton was nowhere to be found.

And yet, after two or three days of this fun out of the sun, Savvy wanted to kick herself. She kept looking around every time she heard male laughter or deep-voiced conversations. Had she suffered sunstroke during her time working on deck or on the docks before now? Who cared whether Ashton was there or not? Actually, it was better that he wasn't. It was so much more peaceful.

She didn't miss him, didn't want to be around him. Hadn't thought about him for a second after that kiss. It was absurd to think for even one moment that she'd like to have anything to do with him. All the evidence was telling her was that he was back with his stupid, ill-mannered, self-centered fiancée. His shoddy fiancée. It was where he should be.

He'd had no business fooling around. And Savannah couldn't feel shame that she'd allowed him to kiss her, or even touch her. She'd said no, after all. Maybe it had come out breathlessly and maybe she could have put a little more oomph into it, but she *had* resisted the man.

And very soon she was going to be on the ocean, away from land, away from worries. She was pretty sure Ashton wasn't going to be on the voyage with them. That meant freedom; that meant a much-needed break. Though she'd had a break from him for at least half a week, she still was thinking about him constantly — but that would stop! If only she were thinking about Darren. He'd been a great date, but she hadn't yet returned his phone calls. Dang it. She told herself it was because she was busy and she'd be gone for a while. But she at least needed to let the man know that.

However, when Thursday rolled around and she looked up to find Ashton walking down the docks as she stepped out for a breath of fresh air, away from all the cleaning fluids, she couldn't help the way her heart leapt and fluttered inside her chest. A smile even flitted across her lips, though she tried to subdue it.

He was back. And he looked damn good. She could tell herself all day long — and all night long — that she had no right to look at an engaged man, but that didn't keep her from sneaking glances his way. He spoke to a few of his employees, and then he was walking toward her.

Her smile of greeting quickly evaporated, though, because as he approached her, he didn't look pleased at all. What in the world had she done now?

"Did you learn all your duties?" he asked tightly.

She was so shocked by his tone that it took a moment for her to find her voice. And she was still at a loss.

"Yes. Shirley says I'm ready to go on the cruise."

"Good." He waved her off and headed in the opposite direction.

For some reason, Savannah called out to him. "Thank you for giving me this opportunity, Ashton. I really appreciate it."

It was difficult to force the words past her throat, but she managed to choke them out. After all, she was getting to take a voyage into the ocean for a ten-day cruise.

Admittedly, she'd be working and not a guest on this luxury ship. But at least she would be at sea. She didn't care that she was cleaning rooms. Cleaning soothed her, except for the chemicals involved, and she could always rock out with her music while she did it. Plus, most of her evenings were completely free. A summer job didn't get much better than this.

"I needed an extra person; that's all. It's not a reward. An employee quit. You're the replacement."

Damn. She hadn't seen him this grumpy in a while, not since the first day she'd met him. She really hoped he wasn't coming along on the cruise, because she would be more than happy to sail off into the sunset and get the heck away from him while he was playing the evil Mr. Hyde.

"I hope I don't disappoint anyone," she said, a nervous laugh escaping.

He looked her up and down, and it definitely wasn't the saucy once-over that he'd subjected her to in the past. She felt she was coming up short, and that wasn't an enjoyable feeling for someone as driven as she was.

"We'll see how it goes."

Her nerves were shot, but Savvy's spine stiffened. She wasn't about to just stand there and let him treat her like garbage. Nobody deserved that — not even her. She hadn't been the one behaving inappropriately.

"Look, Ashton. I know that a man like you most likely doesn't enjoy rejection, and now you think you need to retaliate, but this is unprofessional of you. I didn't do anything wrong. I just explained myself to you as honestly as I could."

He stopped and looked at her, his expression never changing. Maybe he planned to make her life completely miserable in hopes that she would just quit and he didn't have to risk getting sued for firing her. If he went that way, she would probably be much better off by giving him what he wanted — leaving his company, not having sex with him, of course.

"I'm sorry if you're somehow offended, Savvy," he said before an almost cruel smile ran across his lips. "Actually, I take that back. I really don't care if you think that I'm being inappropriate."

So cold. He was being so unbelievably cold. She was grateful she hadn't slept with the man, because if this was the way he treated women, she wanted nothing at all to do with him. No, thank you.

"Do you want me to quit? Is that what you're trying to get me to do?" She might as well say it, though she was terrified of his answer. She needed the money, and she wanted the ocean.

He was silent for several heartbeats, as if seriously considering what she'd asked him. Then his eyes blazed before he managed to tamp the flames back down.

"No. Then I'd be even more shorthanded. Just do your job and we won't have a problem."

Savvy wanted to slap him, scream at him, push him over the side of the dock, and she wasn't sure in which order she wanted to do all those things. So instead of getting instantly fired by doing one or all three, she decided now was a good time to make her showstopping exit.

So she stomped off. This conversation was getting them nowhere, and she was finished with going in circles. A relieved breath left her when he didn't follow.

She'd just avoid him the rest of the day and then she'd sail off into the seas, getting a blessed ten days away from him. The fates couldn't be so set against her that she wouldn't have this little slice of freedom.

Not even her luck was that bad.

CHAPTER EIGHTEEN

ASHTON FELT LIKE a complete ass. He *was* a complete ass, actually. He was in a lousy mood, and Savvy was a large part of the reason for that, but she didn't deserve the way he'd taken out his wrath on her. Seeing her with another man had set him off and he'd been a complete monster since Saturday night. Her continual rejection of him wasn't helping either.

Then he'd been so irate over that kiss, he'd told himself to leave, only to turn around and make sure she was thinking of no other man than him. But dammit, if he was an ass to her, then it didn't matter how much she desired him, she'd want nothing to do with him. He was spinning in circles, and it was time to stop that.

She wasn't going to speak to him again, let alone spend any amount of time with him. Not that he wanted to spend time with anyone of the female persuasion. Not after what he'd gone through a couple of days ago.

He'd ended it with Kalli, and that hadn't gone as expected. She'd screamed at him for three hours straight. It was enough to make him become a monk. Damn, women could be pissy when they considered themselves scorned. Hell, *pissy* was a freaking understatement. *Hell* was an understatement.

He decided that some nice grunt work would be the best thing he could do, so for the next few hours he did all those tasks he'd been accused — during his more entitled days — of being unwilling or unable to do anymore. And by his own father, who naturally knew best. Damn, he needed to stop with the snide comments, even if they were only in his head.

As the sun rose higher in the sky and the temperature reached the mid-eighties, Ashton felt good. Sweat dripped off him as he pushed himself harder and harder.

After a little while longer, he stripped down to his shorts and dove into the water, instantly cooling his anger down. Okay, the work was helping too. He wasn't nearly as ticked off as he'd been when he'd started busting his ass today.

But just as he was climbing out of the water, he heard a screech, and then a groan from his foreman. Dammit! He knew he'd forgotten something. He hadn't changed the security code for the docks yet, and his former fiancée was moving rapidly toward him.

His men were going to get off on this big-time blowout. And to Ashton's complete joy, he looked over and found Savvy speaking with a couple of the guys and in easy hearing range. Okay, he wasn't quite finished with his sarcastic internal monologue.

"Did you honestly think you could break up with me just like that, sneak out of the hotel when I was in the other room, and believe that would be the end of it?" Kalli yelled, making sure the entire island could hear the depth and the breadth of her outrage.

"I didn't sneak out, Kalli," Ashton told her. "I figured you'd shrieked at me long enough — three hours to be exact, unless you want me to get into minutes and seconds — and you were finished. There was nothing else to say."

"What? Nothing else to say? Does this ring on my finger look like nothing, Ashton? You promised me marriage and that's exactly what you'll give me. You will *not* walk away from me. We're talking breach of promise."

"Kalli, it's over, and in this century you can't really think that you'd win a lawsuit of that sort. You need to accept that and move on. Keep the ring, as I've already told you. Hawk it, reuse it, do whatever the hell you want to do with it, but we *are* over. You need to accept that and leave." Ashton was trying to remain calm, but this woman had no business creating a scene in front of his crew.

"Ashton, you can't do this to me. You can't," she said, no longer snarling as the waterworks began.

"I'm sorry I hurt you, Kallista. I really am. If I did hurt you. But you have to admit that we weren't a good match. Hell, both of us were far happier when we weren't together." He felt compelled to remind her of that, even in front of this growing throng of eager eavesdroppers.

"That's not true, Ashton. It's not true at all." She was shedding copious tears as she glided toward him.

He retreated slowly. "No, Kalli. Don't do this. This is where I work. You've already created more of a scene than you should have. So let this go."

"Let's go talk in private, baby. I have some things to show you."

"Kalli, please don't make me get security to escort you out of here. I don't want to embarrass you that way, but if you don't leave on your own right now, you're going to leave me no choice."

Out of the corner of his eye, he saw Savvy begin to move from the ship she was working on and start going up the docks. Dammit. He wished she'd been able to stay out of Kalli's sight. Was he born cursed?

The ex-fiancée spotted Savvy at just that moment. Yes. Cursed.

"It's because of that bitch, isn't it?" Kalli screeched, her tears immediately disappearing. The woman could turn them on and off faster than a working faucet.

"This has nothing to do with anyone but you and me," Ashton told her. "And I'm done talking to you. I've already explained your choices: turn around and leave, or be escorted out." He was fed up with humoring her.

When she didn't move immediately, he nodded his head to a security man who was standing by.

"Don't bother, Ashton. I know my way out." Then, thankfully, she turned on her expensive heels.

He hoped like hell she didn't trip again in this new pair.

He didn't need to watch her as she left in a huff. He was finished with the woman he'd agreed to marry, and he didn't give a flying … damn. What in the world had he been thinking? Arm candy and perfect trophy wife, plus a good set of business connections? That just wasn't worth the headache of marriage.

But he suddenly heard another screech of rage and he spun around in time to see Kalli lunge and shove Savvy, who was standing there completely unprepared.

With no time to react, Savvy flew backward and splashed into the cool water. The security guy went after Kalli, who was now gripping her dangerous heels in her hand while running up the dock.

Ashton didn't have time to deal with that mess. He rushed over to the water, dove in, and grabbed Savvy just as her head resurfaced.

This time she didn't fight him as he pulled her to the ladder and gave her a push to help her get up. And then he found himself there in front of her, both of them soaked, her face in shock.

And he couldn't stop the words that popped out. "Haven't we met here before?"

Her eyes widened for a moment and then her lips twitched and that was all it took. Suddenly both of them were bent over with laughter. His crew would surely think he'd gone mad, but they were all smart enough to stand back and pretend not to watch the new episode of this soap opera.

"This so isn't funny," Savvy finally gasped.

"No, I know," Ashton had to agree. And then he couldn't drag his gaze away from her sparkling eyes. "Damn, I want to kiss you right now."

She retreated if just a step. "Don't you dare," she whispered. "The rest of the crew most likely already thinks of me as a homewrecker, and you know my sentiments about that."

"I guarantee you that if they think you're the reason that Kalli and I broke up, then they're planning a party in your honor, with balloons and confetti. She wasn't particularly well-liked around here. Or so I've been told recently."

"That's a terrible thing to say, Ashton, absolutely terrible. She was obviously hurting from your breakup to have come down here."

"Um, she did just push you into the water. And you're defending her? I don't think I'll ever understand the way women think."

"That wasn't particularly kind of the woman — downright mean, to tell the truth. But she's not thinking straight. She's in pain," Savvy said, making his mouth drop open.

"That's the difference between the two of you, Savvy," he said. "You have a heart. She doesn't. She's pissed because she loses access to my bank accounts and the megabucks in them."

That stopped whatever she'd been about to say — she stood there gaping at him. Her eyes widened at his comment about money, but it wasn't a look of greed he saw, but a look of fear. She took another step away from him. Interesting. Everything about her was interesting.

"Come on. I'll get you a towel," he said, holding out his hand.

She took another step back. "I sooo don't think so. That's how this whole disaster got started."

It took him a moment and then he was smiling again. Damn if she hadn't pulled him out of that grouchy mood of his. He really was falling for this woman.

"Aw, come on, angel face. Maybe this time when we fall, I'll actually get to complete the kiss," he said with a wink.

"Oh my gosh, Ash, I can't believe you just said that," she whispered before looking around. Of course everyone was staring at them, and her cheeks glowed with the brightest of reds. "I'm out of here." She wheeled around and scurried away from him.

He thought for a few seconds about pursuing her. After all, she would be rushing to her bathroom and stripping off her sodden clothes. Dammit! Just like that he was growing a raging hard-on. Yeah, maybe it was best if he let her warm up and cool off at the same time.

Still, he ignored the knowing glances of his crew members as he walked past them whistling. His day had gone from crap to pretty great in a matter of minutes. There was just something amazing about Savvy that did that to him.

He was more than looking forward to the next ten days. Savvy couldn't run from him in the middle of the sea.

CHAPTER NINETEEN

S AVVY WATCHED A crowd form at the departure docks, located about a mile away from where she normally worked on the boats. True, she was going to be working like mad on this cruise, but she couldn't help but feel the rush of excitement from the obviously upscale folks getting ready to board.

It was a red-carpet ride all the way from the get-go. Tents were set up so Ashton's guests didn't have to swelter in the sun. Refreshments were out, and there wasn't a single person there who didn't seem to be smiling.

Ashton was nowhere to be found, and Savvy was now confident he wasn't a part of this voyage. She felt as if a twenty-pound weight had been taken off her shoulders. Ten days at sea was just what the doctor had ordered for her to get over her fascination with this man.

Yep, she would be healed for sure.

Despite the crush of people, the process went smoothly, as guests were each handed a packet that included their itinerary, dining options, room keys, and the layout of the ship — including how to get to their rooms or suites. Savvy sure as heck hoped they enjoyed their rooms. She and a lot of other staff members had left roses on the pillows along with a tote bag filled with essentials that a lot of passengers tended to forget, such as sunscreen, lip balm, and makeup remover wipes.

Savannah hadn't ever been on a real cruise — she'd never even been to a resort, nice or not so nice — but she was told that Ashton insisted that the Storm adventures be VIP for every single passenger. They were paying for it, and he wasn't about to rip anyone off. So as much as Savvy didn't want to like or appreciate the guy, she had to respect him as a business owner.

In each cabin, she and others had also set out a bottle of champagne on ice, and a tray with cheese, crackers and fruit, so passengers could get settled in and have a snack before they began searching for an early dinner.

"Savvy, time to get aboard."

Turning away from the last passengers loading, Savvy followed her co-worker through the back entrance of the ship and decided to watch from the private back deck when they pulled the anchor and began sailing out to sea.

Her disappointment at not seeing Ashton — wait! She wasn't disappointed! — was soon pushed aside as the next hour rushed by and then they were casting off. There wasn't anything to do for the rest of the afternoon but prepare to enjoy the scenery as the ship made its way up the Pacific Coast. The first stop she'd get a chance to get off the ship would be in Skagway, Alaska. Passengers got a full day and night at most of the stops. Some even chose to stay in hotels on the islands just to experience more of the area.

Savvy couldn't understand why they'd pay for another room when they already had one, but apparently people with money didn't mind wasting it. Whatever. She decided not to think like that. It wasn't the judgmental mood she wanted to set for herself.

"Is this a first time for you?"

Jumping a bit at the question, Savvy turned to find Weston standing next to her, and though it had been several days since he'd last flirted with her, he seemed to be on his game right now as he sent her a sultry look.

"Yes, it's my virgin voyage. One day I would love to be a real guest on one of these cruises, and especially this one, considering the way those lucky people are treated."

He moved a little closer, and his shoulder was brushing hers as they watched the boat begin pulling away from the dock.

"Yeah, Mr. Storm gives each of us a free trip after we've been here a year, but honestly, we also get a lot of time off during these trips, so I haven't taken one yet as a passenger," Weston told her. "I enjoy working, and, man, do I make a lot of tips!"

"That's because you work in the casino, Wes. I would love to do that job. I think I'd be a killer blackjack dealer. I've played a lot of it on my phone," she said, and tossed him a wink.

"Talk to the boss. He likes to give everyone a variety of opportunities."

"Maybe on another ride. Anyway, I don't think I'll be on too many. I'm only here for the summer."

"Why's that?" he asked.

"I go back to grad school in the fall, and I can't disappear for another ten days after classes have started."

"Want to meet me here tonight? I'm off at two in the morning."

Savvy wanted to groan. No, she didn't want to meet up with him, but she also didn't want there to be any awkwardness between her and any of her co-workers. Plus, she really did enjoy the flirting. Was that her little sister's influence? It had to be.

When she remained silent for several moments, his beautiful smile fell away, and she searched desperately for something to tell him.

"I would love to, Weston, but I have to be up early, so I'll be out cold by the time the casino closes," she said. At least she wasn't lying to the man. She would be in bed by midnight at the latest.

He seemed disappointed but by no means devastated. "Do you have the early shift all through the cruise?"

"Yes, I'm sorry."

"Me too. I'm sorry, I mean. I work late, so I sleep in. Maybe we can catch lunch or something."

But even as he said it, she saw him look down at the lower deck, and his eye was caught by a woman who was walking by in a skimpy blue dress.

"Go get her, Casanova, before Mark does," Savvy said, pointing out another co-worker who also had a lustful eye on the blonde.

Weston barely mumbled goodbye before taking off, and Savvy blew out a sigh of relief. The crisis had been averted.

She stayed where she was as long as possible and enjoyed the warm sun on her face. Then work called again. Turning too quickly, she had to grab the railing before she slammed down on the floor. There weren't even any waves she could blame for her near fall, dang it. But she forgot all the awkwardness of the past hour as she had to shuffle from cabin to cabin to deal with the passengers' requests.

The regular dinner hour came and went without her having the chance to eat, and she was more than ready to make an early night of it. She was dead on her feet and starving. Good thing there was granola and juice in the break room. She could grab some and eat in her bed — screw the crumbs.

The next day was exactly the same. Shirley assured her that they worked fewer hours once at port and not getting calls from the passengers every two minutes. But the first two days of the cruise were always the hardest as people began clamoring for all the things they'd forgotten to pack, and that sometimes went into the underwear department. Sheesh.

By the end of the day, she tried to be as inconspicuous as possible as she snuck through the crowds. She didn't want to be asked for anything by a single soul. The stairs were in sight … when someone grabbed her arm.

"The captain has requested that you sit with him for dinner."

She didn't recognize the man who'd just spoken to her and she stiffened.

"Why in the world would the captain want to dine with me? I think you have me mistaken for someone else," she told him, tugging against his hand.

"No, Ms. Mills. The captain asked specifically for you."

And then Savvy knew why she hadn't seen Ashton the day before. He'd been onboard already. *He* was obviously playing the part of the captain on this cruise. She'd never know how she'd gone along happily for thirty-six hours without figuring out that minor detail.

All she knew for sure was that the next several days of peace she's so desperately wanted had just sunk deep down into the bottom of the ocean.

CHAPTER TWENTY

PACING BACK AND forth through his suite, Ashton wondered what in the hell he was doing, and not for the first time. He'd purposely avoided Savvy since the day before the ship set off because he'd decided he wasn't going to keep going after a woman who obviously wasn't interested. A woman who could make out with another man on *his* docks. A woman who so openly flirted with the men *he* hired.

He'd been incredibly proud of himself when he hadn't summoned her the first night of their voyage. That had required some restraint — intense restraint — but he'd done it. Now, on the second night out, he wasn't quite so in control of his baser instincts. He'd sent one of his men to find her.

He should have had her reassigned to another ship, made sure that the two of them wouldn't be stuck out at sea together in fairly close quarters, with no possibility of escape. But had he done what his better brain had told him to do? No. He seemed to have lost several million brain cells in the past six weeks.

He was a moron. That's what it was. It was either that or he was just a glutton for punishment, and he wasn't a masochist, was he? Either way, this wasn't bound to go well. Bound ... Hmm ... Nope. Not having a thought like that.

When a knock sounded, he actually felt his heartbeat kick up a few paces. That only served to piss him off more. He moved purposefully to the door and thrust it open. And then she was standing there, and all he wanted to do was pull her into his arms.

Somehow he managed to stop himself.

"Thanks, Ricky," he said in his most controlled voice. "That will be all for the evening."

His guard disappeared, and Ashton led Savvy into the room. She wasn't quite kicking and screaming, but she appeared far from happy.

"I didn't realize you were on the ship," Savvy said, standing uncomfortably in the entranceway of his large suite.

"I run the boats. Where else would I be?" he asked her.

"You have more than one boat, Ashton," she pointed out. "Or should I call you Captain Stubing? Is this your version of the Pacific Princess, the *Love Boat*?"

"Are you going to act cranky all night?" he said as he moved over to the dining table, which was set and waiting.

"I didn't ask to come here," she told him. And if her eyes had narrowed before, they were like slits right now.

"You've been invited to dine with the captain. That's an honor," he said, knowing that would irritate her further. He was right. Normally, of course, the captain dined in the main room with the passengers, but he was in no mood to subject his guests to his presence on this particular evening. Not good for business.

"Seriously, Ashton, what in the hell are you doing?" she asked. "I've had a long couple of days and I'm exhausted.

"I wanted to dine with you. Since you're here and probably hungry after those *long* days of yours — part of them spent watching the water — why don't we try to get through the meal with as much civility as possible? Was that phrased properly for a woman of your education?"

She looked toward the door, and then at the set dining table, and then back at the door, as if trying to decide what to do. As much as it would pain him, he decided that if she turned and left, he wouldn't chase her. After all, he had nine full days to get her to come to him before the boat got back home.

"Oddly enough, I *am* hungry," she said, and took a tentative step toward the table.

"Good. The same goes for me."

He moved to her chair and held it out. She eyed him warily for a moment, but eventually moved forward and sat down.

"Still, I can't be out too long, Captain. I have an early morning."

He grinned. "I could probably get you excused. I know the boss."

"I'm not asking for special treatment, Ashton. I want to do my job and not tick off my co-workers."

"All righty, then," he said. "Why don't we just enjoy a nice meal and save the fighting for another day?"

Her mouth dropped open at that comment. "*You* are the one who's been in a bear of a mood for a while now."

"You're absolutely right," he told her, taking satisfaction in the shock in her eyes. "You've turned me down so many times now that I can't even count them anymore. You've done a damn good job of wounding my pride."

"What?" she gasped.

Leaning toward her so she was sure to hear every word he was saying, and to have no doubt about what he wanted, he waited until he had her full attention. "I like you, Savvy. I like you a lot. I no longer have a fiancée — you saw that little melodrama play out. No one is coming between us, and we're now on this ship for more than a week. I'm going to pursue you, and I'm not going to stop, because I firmly believe that you like me too."

After delivering that little speech, he leaned back, feeling pretty good. It was much better to get that out right away. Flirting was great and all, but there was nothing quite like honesty. Up front, up close, and personal.

Before she was able to reply, one waiter came in and filled their wineglasses while another one set down bread and salad. Then both men disappeared.

"Why me?" she asked him.

That floored him. What could she mean by that? But as he looked at her, he started to glimpse the hint of insecurity in her eyes. Did she really not understand how fascinating she was? How incredibly beautiful?

There was no possible way, he thought. But as he continued to study her, he realized that she really must not know her own value. If he were a complete rogue, he would use that to his advantage. But the mere thought of hurting her in that way disgusted him.

"I can't think of anyone or anything other than you, Savvy. Everything about you has my world spinning out of control. I feel that if I don't spend time with you, I'm never going to be the same again." Quite a rare admission for him, one that offered up to her a piece of his own well-hidden vulnerability.

"... Ashton —"

He interrupted her before she was able to finish that statement. "Are you thirsty?"

"Well ... um ... yeah," she had to admit.

He stood up from the table and walked behind his bar. He pulled out a couple of different bottles of liquor and enjoyed her smile when he tossed two bottles in the air, caught them perfectly, and then poured a bit of vodka and a bit of tequila in her frosted glass. With a little spin, he then grabbed the gin, and added some of that before taking the glass and scooping ice into it, adding a splash of rum, and some Sprite. Putting a cherry on top, he moved over to her.

"What is this?" she asked with a frown.

He grinned as she took a sip and scowled. "It's called the *leg spreader*," he said with a chuckle.

"Ashton, I prefer wine," she said, and she pushed the glass away.

He wasn't offended at all. With a laugh, he removed her glass and got a nice bottle of wine. He then watched her as she downed an entire glass, and, gentleman that he was, he refilled it for her. Obviously, she needed some liquid courage to get through the evening. Didn't everybody from time to time? He surely had.

"Now, let's get back to talking about the two of us," he said, feeling more relaxed than he thought he should considering the circumstances.

"I just really don't think it would be a good idea for you and me to ... well ... you know."

And right then Ashton decided to change tactics. He was more determined than ever to have this woman, but obviously his strong-arm tactics weren't working with her. The wheels continued to spin in his head as he sat back and watched this intriguing woman play with her soup — letting the liquid drip from her spoon without taking a bite.

He was a businessman, and he had to remember that. If one method continued to fail, hit a brick wall — even out at sea, where brick walls weren't heavy on the ground — it was time to try something new. And Ashton had never been one to give up on anything.

So he stopped talking about how he felt about her, and instead began quizzing her on how her day had gone. He couldn't miss the turmoil raging inside her.

She was his. She just didn't know it yet.

CHAPTER TWENTY-ONE

WOULD SHE EVER have any sense of balance around this man? She was feeling a bit seasick, and the sea had nothing to do with.

Ashton was chatting away companionably about captaining the boat, and telling her how one of his crew members had almost fallen into the water when they cast off from the dock, among other topics from the past two days. Who cared? She certainly didn't. What she cared about was this brand-new attitude of Ashton's. Who was he now?

He had gone from brutal Mr. Hyde back to civilized Dr. Jekyll, and he was being far friendlier than he'd ever been. And she was feeling herself give in to him. It seemed impossible to fight both him and herself. And now there wasn't a fiancée standing between them.

Even if Savvy knew that she'd be nothing more than a conquest for him, would it be so wrong for her to enjoy the fruits of his labor? After all, she was a twenty-four-year-old virgin. Wasn't it high time she experienced what everyone else seemed to think was so damn grand? Maybe the earth would really move … except that they were on the ocean. Details, details.

When Ashton had been trailing his kisses down her body, she'd certainly felt something she'd never felt before. And even when she was angry with the man, her body didn't seem to get the message.

"I think I've probably had a bit too much wine," Savvy finally said as she set down her glass and tried to focus in on whatever Ashton was saying.

It had to be the wine that was sending all these thoughts through her head. It couldn't be that she wanted to be just another of his one-night stands.

"You've only had a couple of glasses, Savvy," he pointed out.

Damn! He was keeping track. She was so nervous right now that her fingers were shaking. She could do her darnedest to blame it on the wine, but she knew the real reason all too well — it was simply being in his presence. And her awareness that he was now available was a heady rush that was shutting down her system.

Was she going to continue to live with regret? Did she really want to be that girl who always played by the rules? A girl, or even a woman, ruled by her fears? How fun a life was that? Not much fun at all, according to her sister, who was younger but sometimes wiser.

As she and Ashton chatted about nothing in particular and certainly nothing deep or supercharged, Savvy couldn't help but let the protective walls that she'd erected around herself come down a little bit more and then a little bit more beyond that. She stopped gulping the wine, and instead took small sips.

If she decided to share a bed with this man, she refused to make alcohol the villain. She wouldn't tell herself in the morning that she'd done it because she'd been inebriated. She wanted to own her decision — whatever that decision was going to be.

Their meal was now finished and Ashton stood up. Maybe she didn't have to make any decisions, she thought with something bordering on disappointment. Their night appeared to be over.

But Ash didn't lead her to the door. He ushered her into another room, a small sitting area with a couch, a recliner, a television, and even a gas fireplace, which was already burning.

The lighting was turned down low, and Savvy didn't protest when he grasped her hand gently and led her to the couch. He sat down and tugged her onto his lap. Oh, it felt far too good.

He said nothing as he leaned her head back so he could look into her eyes. There was a question in his, and she knew what he was asking. This was the big moment. She had to decide whether she was going to do what she wanted — or do what she knew would be smart.

When she felt his hardness pressing against her backside, a sigh escaped her throat, and she enjoyed the thrill of watching his eyes ignite. Testing this new power, this emerging sexuality surging through her, she wiggled her hips against his arousal, and he responded with a low groan.

"If you're going to play with me, Savvy, you should be aware that I always win," he growled. His hand came up and he clasped her hair, pulling her head back before he bent and kissed her throat — just a light trace of his lips and tongue against her skin.

She only wiggled her hips again in reply as her core heated and her heart pounded. Yes. She wanted this. But she wasn't sure how to say that to him. She didn't want to tell him she'd changed her mind. She just wanted him to kiss her, and for the next step to follow naturally. Spontaneously? She wasn't sure, but she didn't care anymore.

"I'm going to pick you up now and carry you into my room," Ashton warned her. "If you want this to stop, Savvy, you will have to say so explicitly."

And then she whimpered when he scooted out from beneath her, but she wasn't apart from him long before his arms were sliding beneath her legs and he was lifting her up against the taut contours of his chest.

He stood there for a moment, doing nothing more than gazing down at her lovely face and those limpid eyes. She felt no desire to use words in this moment. But all too soon, his lids drooped and then he was bending forward as he took her lips. And this time she didn't even think about not kissing him back.

She wrapped her arms around his neck and held on tight as he plundered her mouth, his lips making promises she hoped he would keep.

It was too soon when he was letting her go, and then Savvy found herself lying on the side of his king-sized mattress as he stood before her. Damn, he was a beautiful man. Anticipation was flowing through her. Not even an ounce of regret or indecision assailed her. She wanted this man, and she was going to have him tonight. All of him.

"Yes, Ashton," she finally whispered, barely even aware of doing it.

He slowly began unbuttoning first his shirt, and then his trousers. Savvy's mouth dried up as she waited to see him in all his glory, and when he finally stood naked before her, she realized that the wait had well been worth it. He had the type of well-honed body only achieved by a man who wasn't afraid of physical labor. His shoulders were broad, his chest perfectly muscled, and his abs — oh, those abs — were worthy of an A-list action star.

The rest of him ... wow, the rest of him. His manhood stood out thick and hard, smooth satin over solid steel, and mouthwateringly gorgeous. She wasn't sure what she wanted more — to taste him or to have him buried inside her — neither of which she'd ever done or felt before.

"You're magnificent," she moaned.

"Ah, sweet Savvy, you are the one who is magnificent."

Making quick work of it, he stripped her clothes away, and then he was the one moaning as he looked at her from head to toe before he began kissing his way down her body, his lips barely touching her skin before he moved to a new part of her.

"You're flawless, Savvy, more perfect than I even imagined," he told her as he slowly made his way back up to face her. "I can't seem to taste enough of you."

"I have many flaws, but I'm grateful you don't seem to see them," she said. For only the briefest of moments was she self-conscious about lying beneath this inimitable man. He was looking at her with such adoration that she didn't have time to develop her standard fears and insecurities.

He refused to acknowledge the nonsense of what she'd just said, and did the classic thing. He stopped her from even thinking such absurd thoughts by not only kissing her but also pressing his naked body intimately against hers.

Winding her hands around his back, she clung to him and circled one leg around his back. It all felt so right, so perfect, much more perfect than she'd imagined this moment would be.

As she arched her hips upward, he broke the kiss, a kiss that was making her go out of her mind. What was he doing now? She found out quite soon. With a small smile he grazed his lips across her jaw and flicked his tongue out to savor her heated skin, and he slid slowly down her neck and over the mounds of her breasts.

Licking and nipping at each nipple, he didn't move on until she was groaning beneath him, and then he did some serious navel-gazing. Her belly was rippling at this point, and everything went into overdrive. He was spreading her thighs wide open and nibbling along the inside of each of them.

Savvy cried out when the first swipe of his tongue touched the hottest part of her body. Sensations she hadn't known existed traveled through her as he pushed her thighs even farther apart and then ran that amazing tongue along the seam of her heat.

"Ashton …," she almost wept. Did she want him to continue or to stop? It was too much. The burning in her core was making her stomach grow tighter and tighter. Her legs were trembling and her head was thrashing against the bed as she struggled against such an unfamiliar loss of control.

"Don't fight me, Savvy. Just enjoy this," Ash said before burying two fingers deep inside her while he circled her swollen bud with his tongue and sucked on it.

And then something happened inside Savvy that she could barely comprehend. Her core heated to boiling and then exploded. Fireworks. Every muscle of hers shook, she arched off the bed, and she screamed in joy.

As wave after wave of immeasurable pleasure washed through her, she was vaguely aware of Ashton sliding upward on his bed, caressing her all the way. He spoke, but his voice sounded as if it came from a distance, and she couldn't focus on his words.

"You are stunning," he gasped. "I have to take you now while you look like this."

There was no more warning than that. Suddenly he was gripping her backside, and he thrust inside her, his hips slapping against hers.

Sensation after sensation washed through her. If she'd been coming hard and fast before, this was on a new level. Her core gripped him tightly. Yes, she also felt a slight sting of pain as her virgin body tried to adjust to his length and his girth. But the pleasure was so much greater than the pain, and she gave in to the utter ecstasy of it all.

"Damn, Savvy, you're so tight," he groaned as he pulled back and thrust into her again.

This drew another cry of pleasure from her. And as he began moving, faster and faster, her orgasm never quite ended. Just as she was beginning to feel as if she were touching down on earth again, the heat rebuilt.

Her eyes widened as she looked up at Ashton's ravishingly handsome face. And then she shuddered around him again. Though it hardly seemed possible, the pleasure was even more intense than it had been before. Crying out again, she held him close, her nails digging into his back. His voice joined hers as he buried himself deep inside her and they both shook in completion. They were now one in the most intimate way possible.

They were spent, and it took a long, long time before either of them could even think of moving. Or could even think, period. But he ultimately slid off her, and she whimpered her discontent until he pulled her against his side.

"I can't even describe how amazing that was, Savvy," he told her as he traced his fingers along her gleaming back.

"Ditto," she murmured.

Why in the world had she waited so long to experience something that amazing? She was in deep danger now of becoming a hard-core sex addict. She already wanted to do it again — heck, she was thinking of a twelve-step program, but not one of withdrawal.

But he had worn her out with his efforts. Her eyes drifted closed and exhaustion pulled her under. Maybe it would be better to get some rest first. Sex took a lot of energy, and she wanted to be fully alert for round two. And round twelve.

CHAPTER TWENTY-TWO

ASHTON STRETCHED OUT his arm and reached for Savannah, but encountered nothing but empty sheets beside him. Just as he was wrenching his eyes open, he heard the distinct sound of the door to his suite clicking shut.

Though Savvy had tried to do it quietly, some actions just resonated. Yet it didn't dampen his mood. It wasn't as if she could get away from him. They were halfway to Skagway, but for now, they were in the middle of the sea. Unless she wanted to swim like an Olympic champion or even better, she was pretty much stuck here in his territory.

And on the morning after the incredible night before, he had no intention of letting her get too far away from him. He'd heard the expression "best sex I've ever had." But this was better, probably the best sex that *anyone* had ever had. Okay, he couldn't know that. But it was definitely his best sex in all his years. And Ashton was a bit ashamed to admit, even to himself, that he'd had a lot of sex over the years.

Throwing back the covers, he leaped from the bed and headed to the bathroom. And he soon found himself singing in his nice hot shower. Damn, he felt good. But as he stood beneath the spray, he got a visual of Savvy writhing beneath him, and instantly he was hard again — painfully hard.

"Down, boy," he murmured as he switched the faucet to cold and stood shivering beneath the spray.

It took a while, but finally his body began to behave. Sure, he could have taken himself in hand, so to speak, and relieved those uncomfortable tensions, but why in the world would he want to do that? Savvy was so damn close to him on this ship, and he'd much rather do it all with her.

After jumping from the shower, he wrapped a towel around his waist and went back to his bedroom. As he walked to his closet, he turned toward his bed and then stopped. He'd almost missed it in his haste to find Savvy. But now that he'd spotted the evidence, there was no going back. Shock was what he was feeling.

But was this possible? Could he really be seeing what he thought he was seeing? As he stepped up to the bed and looked down, there was no mistaking it. How in the world could he not have noticed? Was he that much of a cad, an insensitive slime?

Blood stained the pure white sheets where he'd apparently taken Savvy's virginity last night. It was beyond belief. But as he sank down onto the edge of the bed and buried his head in his hands, he went over their lovemaking step by step. She'd been so tight, almost painfully so, but he'd been so turned on, and she hadn't complained. He'd figured it had just been a while since she'd shared anyone's bed.

He'd never before had to bear the burden, the responsibility of taking a woman for the first time. What was she thinking now? Had he hurt her? If he'd known, he would have been gentler; he would have given her time to adjust.

No. That wasn't true. Had he known, he would have stopped. He didn't want to be the man to take a woman's innocence. But even as he thought this, he knew he was lying to himself. He didn't think the boat capsizing could have stopped him last night. He'd never wanted a woman so badly as he'd wanted her.

But why hadn't she told him? And how in the hell did a woman get to age twenty-four without ever having sex? Especially a woman as completely sexy as Savvy Mills ...

Well, dammit, Ashton wasn't going to wait long to find out. The more he thought about it, the more upset he became. Was this a game to her? Was she trying to entrap him? What in the world was going on?

While he threw on his captain's uniform, he grew more and more determined to find Savvy immediately and have a show-down. She was most certainly going to explain herself.

Of course, that wasn't happening. As soon as he emerged from his suite, there were issues that he had to deal with. One after another of his employees bombarded him with problems. Dammit!

The only thing keeping him from snapping at each and every one of those employees, though, was knowing that Savvy couldn't run away. He would get a chance very soon to say whatever he needed to say to the woman who had taken his world and flipped it upside down in an incredibly short period of time.

Hours passed and dusk began to settle before Ashton was able to get a real break. It was now time to find Savvy. Now he would get some answers. And he wasn't going to let this woman hide from him anymore.

As he walked down into the area of the ship where the crew slept, he stopped in his tracks. Because, just like that, another thought hit him, and this one made his legs feel a little bit weak.

If Savvy had been a virgin until last night, and all signs pointed that way, it meant the chances of her being on birth control were slim to none. And for the first time he could remember, he hadn't used protection.

CHAPTER TWENTY-THREE

WITH THE MUSIC in her headphones turned up to full volume, Savvy progressed from one room to the next. She was doing basic cleaning up after the passengers, making beds, and turning towels into cute little animals to set on top of the pillows of the privileged people who were taking this cruise. Normally, she wasn't working nights, but one of the other new girls had developed the flu and Savvy had jumped at the chance to stay busy — and, better yet, to avoid Ashton.

She snuck a few of the chocolates into her mouth while she was occupied with putting most of them into bowls in the passengers' rooms. A woman had to do what a woman had to do. She was delighted to find a few notes thanking her for such a job well done in the past two days.

The evening was ending on a more positive note than she'd expected. Sure, the prospect of seeing Ashton again made her nervous as sin. What if he hadn't enjoyed the sex as much as she had? What if he'd had enough of her after the one night?

That would be tragic. Sure, she was a little sore. The man had woken her up in the middle of the night and taken her on another journey — this one was even more acrobatic — and she'd used muscles that had never been used before.

But the soreness was a price she was more than willing to pay for the amount of pleasure she'd received. If only she weren't such a chicken. She'd been too afraid of turning to look into his eyes and seeing disappointment, so she'd run before the first rays of Alaskan sunlight could seep into his windows. So much for her decision to conquer her dang fears.

Okay, there was more to it. She also hadn't wanted her co-workers on the ship to see her doing the walk of shame from the captain's room. Especially if it was only a one-night stand.

Savvy remembered her college days only too well. Roommates of hers had stumbled into the dorm room, still drunk and sporting the same clothes as they'd had on the night before. Hook-ups seemed to be part of the culture, and the girls had always thought her strange because she had no interest in such things.

But their idea of pleasure hadn't looked all that pleasant, in her humble opinion. Yes, the girls would go on and on about how this man had a magic tongue, and how this one had a package that would need at least two UPS trucks. But she'd also heard stories of complete disappointment. And Savvy was convinced that with her luck, that's how it would end up for her. She'd get the boy who jumped right on, got his jollies off, and then ran for the hills.

Not her idea of a good time.

But she couldn't recall a single bad thing about her long night with Ashton. No. It had been the greatest night she could have ever imagined. And she wanted to do it over and over again.

If she could work up the courage to talk to him, maybe, just maybe, she could win a repeat performance from the guy. For now, though, she was going to do her job and then maybe tomorrow she'd get a chance to go out and explore the city of Skagway. That wasn't cutting and running, she insisted to herself.

A tap on Savvy's shoulder alerted her that she was no longer alone. Pulling out her ear buds, she turned and then sighed in relief.

"Hi, Shirley. Is everything okay?"

"Yes, you're doing a spectacular job. Thank you. I've seen the comments from your passengers, and they all appear delighted," the head housekeeper said.

"That's so nice," Savvy told her. "I only have this room and one more to do and then I think I'm done for the night. Did you need me for anything else?"

"Not at all. Sara is already feeling better, so I'm sure she'll be able to take back over her evening shift tomorrow."

"Thank you! When we port and I'm finished tomorrow morning, the first thing I'm going to do is look for a used-book store. I always find great treasures in them. And then I'm going to see all the sites I can before we cast off again."

"That's wonderful," Shirley said before giving her an assessing look. "There's something different about you this evening." Her boss's words immediately made Savvy's muscles tense.

"Nope. Nothing different," she quickly said.

"Hmm. I'm not buying that. Is it the thought of serious shopping?" Shirley muttered. "No, it can't be that. You have said several times how much you hate to shop, at least for clothes."

"I'm just way excited to be out on the ocean," Savvy said with too much enthusiasm.

You must *really* love the sea," Shirley said. The woman's head tilted and she began to examine Savvy closely.

"Yes, I *really* do," Savvy finally said after shifting nervously on her feet.

"I've never seen such a glow on your cheeks."

Savvy's face flamed at that comment. Yes, she was happy to be out to sea, but the glow on her cheeks had nothing to do with that. Not that she was going to tell anyone.

"Yep. I'm so excited to be here," Savvy exclaimed.

"Hmm. Well, okay, then," the woman said before sending Savvy a way-too-knowing smile, which made her shift again.

"Have a good night, Shirley," Savvy called out as the woman headed away.

"You too, darling. But I have a feeling your night is going to go well, no matter what."

Savvy didn't get a chance to respond — when she could find her voice again, the head housekeeper was gone. So she finished the room she was in and moved on to the last one, a one-bedroom suite.

She was almost free to escape to her sleeping quarters, where she wouldn't have to worry about accidentally running into Ashton. But after she'd powered through her work in the last suite and stepped out into the hallway, her heart lodged up into her throat.

Her luck was just never on the good side of the coin. Leaning against the wall and wearing an impressive scowl was the one man she really didn't want to communicate with at the moment — especially with that look on his face, which she already knew too damn well.

But she couldn't just flee from the owner of the company, so she just stood there, resigned to the fact that she'd have to hear whatever he was about to say. The waiting stretched on for an uncomfortably long time.

"Why didn't you tell me?"

Crap! She knew exactly what he was talking about, but she decided this might be one of those times to play the ditzy girl.

"What do you mean?"

"Savvy, don't do that. Don't play dumb," he said in a stern voice.

"I didn't think it mattered," she replied after an eloquent pause.

"You didn't think it mattered that you were a virgin?"

Gulp. Yeah, so she'd just lied. She'd thought it would really matter. She was just hoping that he might not have noticed. Because she hadn't wanted to have this awkward conversation.

But her back stiffened and her eyes grew steely. It was time to go on the offensive. "Are you saying that you didn't enjoy it?"

He looked at her as if she'd lost her mind. That was a good thing, right? It had to be. He seemed shocked that she would say something like that. If only she were better at reading men!

"Of course I enjoyed it. Yes! I enjoyed it so much, Savannah, that I can't get enough of you. But I could have made it better for you, been more gentle."

She didn't reply for several moments, but he gave her the time she needed. Thank goodness for small miracles.

"Would you have still wanted me if you had known I was inexperienced?" she finally asked.

"Yes, I would have still wanted you," he said. "But I don't know if I would have pushed it," he said, before his cheeks glowed a bit at that unfortunate choice of words. "I mean, I most likely wouldn't have pursued you in the first place. I mean — a virgin!" His hands went in the air as he paced in front of her.

She still didn't know how she was supposed to react to this, but her temper seemed to be right there to save her.

"Well, then, it was a good thing I didn't tell you, because I can't imagine how you could have possibly made it any better. I've heard a lot of stories of it being painful and horrible, but there was nothing horrible about that. It was spectacular," she said. "And now you're ruining it for me. That's pure crap!"

He stopped his pacing and sent her a withering look. But she wasn't afraid anymore. She was just ticked off.

"*You* are the one who chased after me, Mr. Storm. *You* are the one who demanded that I have dinner with the captain. *You* are the one who took my clothes off. Don't you dare stand there now and act like this is all on me," she thundered, beyond caring if anyone happened down the hallway.

At her words, some of his anger seemed to drain away, but she didn't care about that either. She was now pissed off all the way around.

"And what about protection, Savvy? I'm going to assume you aren't on any," he said, but his tone was a lot less intimidating.

Wow. She hadn't even thought once about that. Stupid or what? She did some quick math in her head and blew out a relieved breath. "Don't worry, Ashton, I don't want kids, and believe me, I stand firm on that."

"What in the hell is that supposed to mean?"

"It means that it's not the right time of the month for me to get pregnant," she told him, stepping away.

Her words seemed to deflate his anger again. What had he thought she'd meant? Better yet, she didn't think she wanted to know what was going on in his brain.

"You know what, Ashton?" she snapped. "I think it would be much better for all concerned if you stay on your side of the ship — the elite decks — and I stay on mine — in the steerage."

She didn't give him a chance to respond. She was done for good this time with Ashton Storm and his screwed-up philosophies on sex and on what was and wasn't considered acceptable.

CHAPTER TWENTY-FOUR

THE NIGHT HADN'T been good to Ashton. He'd barely slept a wink because of some feverish plan, repeated in his head every other minute, that he was going to storm down to Savvy's room and carry her back to his. But each time he sat up to do just that, he threw himself back down again on the bed.

She wasn't alone in her room, and he knew the humiliation she would feel if he made it so clear to other employees that the two of them were having sex. That wouldn't end well for him.

So he tossed and he turned and he stewed. By the time he had to get out of bed, the ship was getting ready to port in Skagway. It was time to help ensure the safety of his passengers, his crew, and his boat. He would then finish what he and Savvy had started two days before. This time she wasn't escaping him. If she really thought things were over between them, she wasn't as bright as her university transcripts made her seem to be.

By late morning, the ship was pretty much empty, just crew members scattered around cleaning up plus a few passengers who weren't feeling well and didn't want to go out on a lengthy excursion.

Savvy wasn't hard to track down.

He pushed open the door to the room she was cleaning, and any and all words he'd been about to utter froze on his tongue. Ashton was instantly transfixed by the sight before him. Obviously, this woman had him under a spell, and, dammit, he didn't want to find an antidote.

Her finely formed hips were swinging as she stretched high to wipe dust off a shelf, and she was belting out the lyrics to a song he didn't know. The voice was off-tune, but who would notice? When "the hips don't lie" came from her throat and she swung her butt in a perfect spiral, he agreed. The hips most certainly weren't lying.

All his anger and frustration from the day before seemed to grow smaller and smaller the longer he stood there, growing bigger and bigger, in a trance at how much he lusted after this woman.

He didn't make a sound as he watched her sway; he just enjoyed the moment as she danced over to the windows and sprayed some glass cleaner on them. She wiped with her hands in perfect rhythm while those hips kept on gyrating.

He was harder than he'd been in the shower yesterday morning. Damn, he wanted to take her, and right now. Bend her over, flip up the back of that little uniform, take her panties down, and slide it right in. Into that amazing heat of hers. Tight and luscious. He took a step forward.

When she bent over, her ass in the air, forming a perfect cushion for him to slip inside her core, he decided he'd delayed long enough. Turning quickly, he locked the deadbolt to make sure of their privacy and then stepped forward again with purpose.

She was still unaware he was in the room, and this gave him a major advantage. She was bent down when he approached her, cupped those swaying hips with his greedy hands, and pressed against her firm behind.

Savvy screeched. She jumped up, the back of her head nearly slamming into his jaw. He was grinning when she turned around with one hand clutching at her chest and the other at her throat.

Ripping the headphones out of her ears, she scowled at him — he didn't have a monopoly on that expression. "What in the world are you doing, Ashton? You nearly gave me a heart attack."

"I came to hash it out with you some more, and then you took my breath away by the way you've been moving around." He wound his arms around her back and tugged her against him.

"Ashton, this isn't the time or the place ..."

He could see that she wanted to stay mad at him, but the connection they had was just too damn strong. It was a curse and a blessing all in one. She didn't fight against him as he began backing them both up until she was up against the wall.

"This is the perfect place. Everyone is off the ship, and if I don't sink inside you in the next few minutes, I think I'm going to die," he told her. "We will talk soon," he added after pressing his arousal against her.

Then he leaned down and kissed her, his heart racing when her tongue came out and tangled with his and she wrapped her hands around his head to bring him closer.

A growl escaped his throat as he reached for her uniform and worked tirelessly to undo it. And then he reached those dainty panties and pushed them down her legs. He wanted her so badly he was afraid he wasn't going to be able to hold himself together.

Wrenching his head back, he tried to regain some control. "Give me a second, Savvy," he groaned.

Her eyes widened at his evident passion. Once his breathing had returned to somewhere nearing normal levels, he switched positions with her. He was the one now leaning against the wall, but his hands were still gliding over the smooth skin of her ass.

"Oh, Ash, I don't think I will," she said, surprising him.

And then she dropped to her knees and his fingers trembled when they sank into her hair. "You don't have to do this, Savvy," he gritted out as she began undoing his trousers. Not that he would stop her if she insisted.

"I want to taste you, Ash," she said. Her voice was almost shy, barely above a whisper.

Everything about her was so damn hot, her voice, her body, her taste, her scent. And as she freed him from the confinement of his pants and took him in her fingers, he nearly wept with anticipation.

But never in his life had Ashton felt as weak as when her beautiful lips circled the tip of his arousal and she took him inside the recesses of her mouth. A groan thundered from his throat.

She licked and sucked him, and her fingers squeezed him tight. Her head moving up and down along his thickness was the most erotic thing he'd ever witnessed. And the soft moans of appreciation escaping her throat vibrated against him.

He tugged too hard on her hair in his passion, and she released him. But he still almost washed her face with his release when he saw his arousal so wet and so close to her swollen pink lips.

"I need to take you now," he said reaching beneath her arms and pulling her up. None too gently, he turned them both around again so her back was pressed against the wall, and he lifted her up high.

Without a second of hesitation, he slammed her down against him, plunging all the way inside her heat. She cried out and wriggled against him.

And that's all it took for him to completely lose control. He dug his hands into her hips and pounded away inside her over and over again. Their cries mingled together, and then he felt her tightening around him, and they groaned in unison as they found ecstasy.

Ashton's legs grew weak. With a sigh, he drew her down to the floor while still buried inside her. She bounced on him a bit, and, unbelievably, he felt himself instantly growing hard again.

"What are you doing to me, Savvy?" he asked as she began slowly sliding up and down on him while he dropped kisses all along her throat.

"I was going to ask you the same thing," she murmured.

"Dammit, I want you over and over. It feels like a hunger that will never end."

She found her rhythm — man, was she a quick learner! — and now she was convulsing against him as she moved. He shuddered at the intensity of it all.

As his lips trailed down her throat, he unbuttoned her shirt and worshipped her beautiful breasts, and he reached down to rub that special spot on her body. She cried out her appreciation. They made love for what felt like an eternity and yet was too short. And when he found his second release of the afternoon, she was right there with him.

Neither of them spoke for several moments. As they fought to regain their breath, she laid her head against his shoulder and he ran his fingers against her smooth back. But he needed to talk to her about what he'd intended to when he'd first walked into the room.

"Are you finished running away from me, Savvy?"

She tensed on top of him, but he didn't allow her to pull away. She was trapped in his arms and that's where she was staying until they were finished.

"Let go, Ash," she demanded.

"Why?" he said calmly as he continued stroking her back. "Am I hurting you?"

A shiver ran through her. "No, you know you aren't. But I can't have a rational conversation with you like ... like this," she spluttered.

"Like what?" he asked, unbelievably growing aroused again.

"You know like what," she said, wriggling on top of him, making his body come alive more and more.

"Just tell me why you're still trying to run from me. I asked a legitimate question of my lover," he said.

She was silent for a few moments. Then she sighed and gave up fighting him.

"I didn't tell you because I was aroused by you and I didn't want you to change your mind about me because you would think I couldn't satisfy you," she finally said, her voice barely above a whisper.

This stopped Ashton's movements. He leaned back and then gripped her chin so she would be forced to look at him.

"Then why fight me so damn much?" he asked.

"Because you … you frustrate me and I'm not very secure about us," she admitted. "I'm afraid that I can't satisfy you for very long."

"After the sex that we've had, can you honestly believe that I'm not aroused by you? That I don't want you endlessly?"

"Well … it seems you're really into it, Ash, but I've heard guys can have sex with anyone at any time."

"Oh, that's so not true, Savvy. I have never in my life been this turned on by a woman," he said as he grabbed her hand and pulled it to his thickening shaft. "And I've never felt like I couldn't get enough before."

Her eyes widened as she squeezed her fingers around him and then a shy smile appeared on those beautiful lips.

"Well, then, if it wasn't bad for you, I wouldn't mind doing it a few more times."

Her cheeks flushed as she said that last bit, and even though he'd just been buried inside her for more than an hour, he was ready to go again.

"Damn, woman, I think that will be more than okay," he said before he kissed her so hard that they both started panting. "But I'm going to wait until tonight. Because, whether you want to admit it or not, I know you have to be sore right now. You're new at this game, and we've been testing your limits."

He looked at her as he said this and she turned her head away from his probing gaze. And he knew he was right. She wiggled against him, possibly testing her newfound powers of seduction. He growled as he moved away and then stood up.

When she looked at his proud manhood and licked her lips, he retreated a few steps before he was tempted to go back on his word.

"You're either an angel come to save me, or a she-devil here to bring me down," he growled before pulling up his pants.

She smiled at him, and he felt her joy deep inside his chest. So beautiful.

"I'm getting you out of here for a while," he said. "We're much safer away from any bedrooms."

This time Savvy giggled, but she wouldn't leave until she was finished dealing with this room. So Ashton found himself helping to clean the suite of one of his guests. Yes, he was grousing about it the entire time, but the looks of pleasure she sent his way made it all worth it.

He was in serious trouble now. He was almost in love with this woman, and afraid he was nothing more in her mind than a teacher in mattress action. Or wall action. Or floor action. Maybe he just had to make her never want to live without him. Impossible? Hardly. He had the tools to satisfy …

CHAPTER TWENTY-FIVE

HER HEART SEEMED to be exploding, and Savvy gripped Ashton's hand in abject terror. She had her limits, and there was just no way she was going to do what he wanted. Not this time. No freaking way!

But she was trying to move on — trying to get over her fears. She'd picked up a lot of them during her unhappy childhood. But the fears she was more interested in getting over were irrational fears, not fears that made perfect sense.

"I don't think I can walk across this thing, Ashton."

"Yes, of course you can. Aren't you the one who told me that you weren't going to live in a world of phobias anymore?"

Why in the world had she told him that? He was taking it far too literally.

"I know I did, but I didn't mean to conquer all of my fears. Because I really sort of like life. Do you think I want to plunge however many feet that thing is above ground to my certain death?"

"Thousands, even millions of people have crossed this with no one plunging to their death. The view is spectacular from the middle," he said. He tugged her hand a bit, trying to get her to move, but he wasn't forcing her. He was letting her know that it was her decision, even if he was going to push her a little.

She wasn't budging. Yes, she was adventurous, and she loved to hike and loved to be on the ocean and loved trying new things. But she wasn't a fan of heights. It wasn't *entirely* rational, and she got that, but, dang it, she was afraid.

They were currently standing at the entrance to the Yukon Suspension Bridge, which goes over the Tutshi River. Whitewater raged along rapidly fifty-seven feet below, and it was reaching up menacingly to snare its victims. Yet Ashton had been trying to get her to cross the dang bridge for the past fifteen minutes.

They'd spent the afternoon and early evening driving the nearly two-hundred-mile round trip from Skagway to Carcross Corner and back. She'd witnessed the famous Dead Horse Trail, the William Moore Bridge — another one she wouldn't cross — bears, sheep, moose, mountain goats, and some of the most scenic views imaginable.

A great moment had been when they'd stopped in Liarsville — her favorite name for a town ever. They'd walked hand in hand through the Gold Rush Trail Camp, and she'd played tourist and bought a few cheap souvenirs before they hit the road again.

They'd talked for hours, laughed, and this was when she'd admitted to him that she wanted to be a braver person, that she didn't want to live her entire life saddled with fear. Dang, one minute she was telling him that, and the next he was hell-bent on ensuring she try to beat those fears quickly. And now Ashton was threatening to ruin her amazing day by trying to get her to cross this damn bridge. Did he not understand basic psychology on getting people past phobias?

"How about this?" he said in his smoothest voice. "You can grip my hand tight, and if you are seriously freaked out after walking ten steps, we will turn around and I'll leave you alone."

She processed his words, and it did feel like a good compromise, but she just didn't want to see the view. Wasn't that what the Web was for? Still, she hated letting her fears rule her. That wasn't a way to live.

"Fine. But if we die on this trek, I will haunt your soul to the end of eternity, Ashton, and that's a promise."

The man was smart enough not to laugh at her, though she did see his lips twitch. Her eyes narrowed even more, and he managed to deep-six that budding smile. Smart man.

Savvy knew that her nails were digging into Ashton's hand, but no matter how much she told herself to loosen her grip, it wasn't happening. However, as she focused on putting each of her feet in front of the other, she realized that she and Ash were halfway across the bridge, and though she could swear they were really rocking the thing, it felt quite stable.

Ashton tried to speak to her, but she just shook her head and picked up her pace. The sooner they finished this, the sooner she'd be able to say she'd faced another fear, had conquered it, actually, and then she would be done.

Ashton tried to stop and admire the view, but she wasn't having any of that silliness. She practically ran to the other side of the bridge, and before she could think about it, she grabbed his arm and moved swiftly back to where they'd begun.

It wasn't until they were on solid ground again that Savvy took her first full breath in what felt like hours.

"Man, that was terrifying, but it was also a rush — a serious rush," she said. "I can't believe I just did that."

"It would have been nice to enjoy the view," Ashton grumbled.

"Go back and enjoy it all you want. But I'm going to the rental car. I'm done with the bridge."

"I wanted to get a picture of us in the middle," he told her.

"Haven't you been here before?" she asked as the two of them strolled toward their car.

"Many times," he said. "But never with you."

And just like that, her heart thudded in her chest. Maybe he was seriously good with feeding lines to all his women, and maybe she was just vulnerable, but this man did make her feel all warm and fuzzy inside.

Savvy could tell herself all day and night that this was just a fling, and that she wouldn't be affected by it. But she knew herself, and she knew she wasn't going to get out of this unscathed. Each moment she was spending with Ashton, she was giving him a little bit more of herself.

She'd known forever that he was dangerous. But she was in too deep now to change directions, so she might as well just hold on for the rest of the wild ride. Hey! She was really facing a major fear of hers!

Once they returned to Skagway, Ashton surprised her by pulling up to a place called the Red Onion Saloon. She threw him a skeptical look.

"What was that look for?" he asked when he'd come around to her side of the car and opened the passenger door. She still wasn't quite used to having a man do that for her, but she liked this gentlemanly side to him, so she'd take it. And he'd insisted.

"I just don't picture you hanging out at a place called the Red Onion," she said.

"Hey. I know this place well, and they have excellent food," he told her as they approached the double doors. "Besides, this once used to be the classiest dance hall and saloon in Skagway — well, and the finest brothel," he added with a wink. "And since you are now a woman of the world — thanks to me, of course — I thought you'd enjoy it."

The leer he sent her made her laugh instead of slug him. "Are you now saying I'm a lady of the night, since I've allowed you to do naughty things with me?"

"Hmm, a few of those things you've picked up on pretty dang fast," he told her.

"You are terrible." She was slightly worried about how much she did love sex. But there was no way she was going to think ill of herself because of it.

"Is this really an old bordello?" she asked before they entered the building. She wasn't quite sure if he was teasing her or not.

"Yep. It was built in 1897, during the Gold Rush days. The upstairs still has the ten cribs, or rooms, that were once used by the ladies."

Now she wasn't sure what she was walking into.

"Wow. I've never been in a real bordello before," she finally said as she looked around wide-eyed at the waitstaff. The women were dressed in vintage outfits right out of the Old West. Savvy was instantly in love with the place.

"I haven't been to a working one," Ashton assured her with a laugh.

"That's in your favor," she said with a sigh of relief. "One thing at least …"

They were seated and Ashton filled her in on the background.

"Ah, a weary man could stop by the place for some whiskey and a dance. Then he would step up to the bar, where they had ten dolls lined up. The customer would choose his woman by selecting the doll that represented her. If the woman was with another customer, the doll would be lying down. When she was finished and ready for business again, her doll was set back up."

"They did it with more than one guy in a night?" she gasped.

Ashton laughed, making her squirm in her seat a bit. "Sorry. I'm not laughing at you. I just love history, so I know a lot about this stuff."

"I love history too, but I guess I haven't gotten much into the Old West or gold-mining times," she told him.

"Okay, some of this is just idle curiosity from my wacky bartending days, and you can find out everything about this on the Web. But things are a little different from what you see on the TV show *Gunsmoke*. Yes, the 'good-time girls' took as many men a night as possible. It was more money for them and more money for the house of ill repute. Wait until I tell you about prostitution during the Second World War."

"Please don't …"

They were interrupted as the waitress came to take their drink orders. And the two of them later took a tour of the upstairs museum, with all its antiques from the Gold Rush period.

When they left the Red Onion, Ashton dragged her over to the Old Timey Photo Shop. He dressed as a lawman, and she played a lady of the night. It was a picture she would treasure forever — when this all ended, as it inevitably would.

By the time the two of them made it back to the cruise ship, Savvy was exhausted, but the day had been more than she could have imagined. She'd been able to see a side to Ashton she'd never seen before — a playful side. A side that told her how easily she could fall in love with the man if she weren't incredibly careful.

If it wasn't too late.

CHAPTER TWENTY-SIX

SITTING AT HER favorite place on the cruise ship — the back, where passengers rarely ventured — Savvy allowed herself the indulgence of a worried sigh.

She wasn't about to deny that the cruise and all its stops at ports had been magnificent so far. Perfect, in fact.

But she and Ashton were living off caffeine and heightened hormones. They made love nightly, sometimes more than once, and though it seemed impossible, the lovemaking continued to grow better and better each and every time.

The ship was now cruising past a huge glacier with giant chunks of ice splashing off into the water below. It was a little frightening even for a fan of the ocean and of shipwrecks. She'd watched the film *Titanic* a few too many times not to be scared.

Come to think of it, that story hadn't had a happy ending. Was that going to be how her story turned out? Yes, it seemed perfect right now, but what happened when the boat made it home? When they returned to the real world? What if Ashton turned out to be as cold as Jack when he drifted down to the ocean floor.

She'd told herself she wouldn't let her fears overtake her, wouldn't let worries cast shadows on her decisions. Ah, but she was in an epic romance, and with all good romances, there were bumps in the road, or on the sea. The passion ran high — and the letdown sometimes was too much to handle.

Taking a deep breath, she tried to calm herself. It was just that her nerves were beginning to spike again as she realized their voyage would soon be over. What was it going to be like when they returned to Seattle? Were they going to go back to being just boss and employee? Was the sex going to be over? As depressing a thought as that was, what was worse was thinking she wouldn't get to laugh with the man anymore.

She'd gotten to see a side of him that he had hidden from her before, and it was a side she really liked.

"What are you so deep in thought about?"

This time, when Ashton found her as she watched the sun go down, she wasn't startled. She sighed as his arms circled gently around her waist and rested on her stomach. Heat rushed through her, even in the coolness of the Alaskan water.

"I was just thinking that our adventure is almost over," she told him with a sigh.

"Maybe this one is over, but it doesn't mean that we are," he told her as he kissed the side of her neck.

She shuddered at his gentle caress. But she had to say, "We haven't talked about what it will be like when we get back."

He was silent for a little while, though he didn't stop paying homage to her charms. And she suddenly didn't care about the future. Her core went molten and she began squirming against him.

"It will be just the way it is now, but instead of exploring Alaska and Canada, I'll take you to some of my favorite places around Seattle and the San Juan Islands." He was now rubbing his hands tantalizingly along her thighs.

"But I start school in a little over a month, Ashton."

"Your university is in Seattle, Savvy. It's not like we're going to be on different continents." And his lips almost made her forget what they were speaking about.

"I know," she said as she leaned back into him. "But I told you that when I'm in school, it's a different world for me. I'm so busy and so focused on improving myself, on succeeding."

She was beginning to think, though, that maybe she'd been wrong about him. Maybe this wasn't just a fling for him if he truly wanted to work through these obstacles and keep on seeing her. She was afraid to hope for that, but she was starting to.

"We'll figure out a way to be together, my sweet Savvy. I love spending time with you. And if it's important to both of us, we'll make it happen."

"This trip and our romance have happened so quickly, and we've spent so much time together naked that we haven't done a lot of talking." Why was she putting this all out there? Was she trying to push him away?

"We have plenty of time to learn everything about each other. I can't get enough of what I do know about you," he said, melting her heart a bit more.

Savvy had to laugh. "You're a very smooth talker, Mr. Storm."

"I've been told that before." He turned her around so her back was against the rail, and he pressed tightly into her.

"I just bet you have," she said. But she forgot the rest of what she'd been about to say when his lips fused with hers.

She barely felt him grip her hips and lift her onto the rail. But she was more than happy when he stepped inside the V of her legs, and then she felt his hardness pressing against her heat.

"It doesn't matter how many times we make love. I feel like a randy teenager the second I'm within five feet of you," Ashton said as he broke away from her lips and trailed his tongue down the side of her throat.

"Well, I have nothing to compare this with, but I feel the same," she said before a small moan escaped her throat.

"I'd better get you inside, Savvy, before a passenger interrupts us."

"You're right, Ash. If we don't go to your room now, I won't be responsible for what happens. Your reputation is on the line, you know."

His eyes narrowed and he pressed his arousal into her for another moment before pulling her down from her perch and stepping back.

"Damn, I want you," he said.

She believed him. "And I love knowing that," she replied.

When she realized she'd been sitting on the rail, high above the water, and hadn't even noticed, she knew she was in more trouble than she'd thought. In this man's presence, all she could feel was love, excitement, and passion. There was so little room for silly fears.

He took her hand and they raced off toward his suite, passing an employee who tried to get his attention. Ashton didn't even slow down. Right now, nothing mattered to either of them except each other.

In a perfect world, it would always be this way.

CHAPTER TWENTY-SEVEN

ANOTHER DEEP SWELL sent the ship careening to the left.

Savvy cringed as she looked over at Ashton, where he and his team of men and women were navigating through the storm.

"We've gotten through the worst of it, darling," Ashton assured her, looking her way.

No, no one on the ship was unaware of their relationship now. And for some reason, Savvy didn't even care about that anymore. She was doing her job, so her romance with the boss wasn't so disgraceful, she assured herself.

"I'm having a hard time believing you," she said with a nervous chuckle as she looked out the giant windows and saw only wall after wall of nothing but foaming salt water crashing virtually in her face. "I should have known better than to go out onto the ocean with a captain whose last name is Storm."

"Oh, that only brings a little bit more excitement," he said. "Thrills, chills, and spills. But in a few more minutes we will be able to make it back down to my suite."

After a few more nail-biting moments, she discovered that he was right, darn him. The waters calmed. There were still some swells, but as she looked out the window, she noticed stars breaking through the cloud cover. Her body began to relax.

For the next little while, his people continued steering the boat through the water, soon allowing the computers to take over, and then she saw more and more stars above them. She didn't notice at first that Ashton was now kneeling in front of her.

"It's all under control, Savvy. We're through the storm, and the passengers have been notified and offered complimentary drinks at the bar tonight — any of them who still have the stomach for it. Let's get out of here and enjoy ourselves. Just the two of us."

He reached for her fingers and peeled them away from the rim of her chair. She hadn't even realized she'd been holding on with such a death grip.

The two of them slowly made their way to his suite, the rocking of the boat a little more intense than it normally was, but nothing like it had been for the past couple of hours.

"I have to admit that wasn't the most enjoyable of the nights I've had on this cruise," Savvy said after Ashton shut the door behind them. "I have a pretty strong stomach, but it's a little stirred up right now."

"The ocean is so much more powerful than most people realize. It does take a lot of lives every year, but I have an incredibly competent group of people working for me, and they'd never let us get into a situation that we couldn't get out of. If we'd been in the middle of the storm, it might have been a different story, but we just caught the edges, thankfully."

Ashton led her to his dining table. He grabbed a bottle, pouring each of them some amber liquid before he joined her. Savvy automatically picked it up, then began sputtering when the liquid burned all the way down her throat.

"What in the world is that?" she said, her stomach feeling like it was on fire.

"It's a nice shot of scotch. Family favorite. I know it burns, but it will help with the nerves. Finish it up."

She decided to trust him and, with a grimace, threw back the rest of the drink. He put cheese and crackers in front of her next, and she swallowed what she could, hoping that the food would help the burning and her upset stomach. It did.

"Now, you can have some more with a mixer," he said as he sat across from her, a drink in his hand.

"Are you trying to get me drunk, Mr. Storm?" she said, feeling much better.

"I'm just showing off some of my mad bartending skills from the good old days," he told her with a laugh as he stood up, grabbed a bottle and tossed it in the air and then caught it after it spun a few times.

"Sexy. Just like Tom Cruise," she added with a wink.

"Hey!" he said with his signature scowl. "I'm much better-looking — and taller — than he is."

"Hmm ..." She paused as his scowl deepened. Then she conceded. "Yes, you are, Ashton."

"That's much better," he told her.

Damn, he looked so good as he leaned back in his chair, a relaxed smile on his lips.

"I have to admit that I was incredibly impressed with the way you were handling the ship. Thanks for letting me go to the control room with you."

"All of the crew have been in storms before and as I said, those storms can be deadly, but if everyone works together, they aren't so bad. Now, if you ever see panic on my face, then is the time to grip your chair and forget to breathe."

"I wasn't exactly looking at your face, Ashton. I was watching the water trying to overtake this little boat. Trying to look taller, like you versus Mr. Cruise."

"*Trying?*" he said with mock outrage. "I never try. "But seriously, storms are actually pretty fascinating to watch if you sit back and think about it."

"Now that I know we're out of danger, I agree with you, it was intense. But I don't think I'll be able to sleep at all tonight. I'm far too wired now."

"Then we'll talk all night if you want. We pull into Seattle tomorrow, so we both get the day off."

"But I still have to clean my rooms, Ash."

"No you don't, Savvy. All the bedding is stripped and we bring in the big guns to prepare the ship for its next cruise."

"I'm not one of the big guns?" she asked with a smile as she flexed her right arm. There was a little muscle there that she was quite proud of.

"You most certainly are, darling."

He led her over to the couch and sat down with her in his arms. She sighed as she leaned into his warmth. This was heaven — right here, right now. With just a few of his words, she felt safer, warmer, and taken care of.

"I have always loved the sea, and I've been able to go out on dives, but never very far out, and only under the best weather conditions. But I've never really gotten to spend days and days at sea. It's been a real treat — storms and all."

"You'll have to come on the next cruise as my date, and it will be easy as sin. We'll have so much more time together."

"Don't you still have to take care of navigating the boat?".

"I have a very reliable staff. They don't even need me in there most of the time," he said.

"Aren't you running yourself out of a job?"

"I own the company. I play captain for fun, and then drive the real professionals crazy in the control room on occasion. But someday I plan to go out on the seas when I have young kids running around. My prime directive in life, I suppose, is to spend time with the people who are most important to me."

"Wow, you really think ahead." She'd instantly lost that relaxed feeling.

He seemed to notice her uneasiness.

"Don't you? Most people I know have plans for their future, Savvy. Why so tense all of a sudden?"

"Oh, I'm not tense. And I do have plans, but they are all related to work," she told him with a nervous laugh.

"Not everything should be about work, Savvy. What about family?"

She was quiet for a moment. "It's just my sister now. Just the two of us."

"That's not the family I'm talking about. What about children?"

She really didn't want to answer this question. She had a feeling they weren't on the same page. They'd barely begun dating. Was this really a topic that should be coming up so fast? Dammit.

"I'm not going to have kids," she finally said. "I have other plans."

She felt him freeze up behind her. And the hand that had been caressing her arm so lovingly was now still.

"I don't mean tomorrow, Savvy. I meant in the future."

She couldn't read his tone of voice. "I didn't have the most wonderful childhood," she told him. "And I don't think I'd make a good mother, so I decided long ago that I will never become one."

He was quiet for so long, she wondered if he was going to speak again. Just when she was about to give up, he gave her an answer.

"Lots of people say that, Savvy, but you can break any cycles you had with your own family. You're caring, compassionate, and the most wonderful woman I know. I know that you'll make a fantastic mother."

"No, Ashton, I won't be a mother. I have *zero* desire to have children. You've seen some of my fears, but this is probably my worst one."

He really needed to understand this. When he pulled back from her, she felt as if a vise was clamping around her insides. This was another reason she hadn't wanted to get into a serious relationship. When men were thinking about marriage, they were also thinking about procreation, weren't they? She didn't understand why. Weren't there enough people in the world already? Why was she considered defective if she didn't want to add to the population?

And did her feelings make her less of a woman? When Ashton stood up and she looked into his eyes, she almost felt that it did. His expression wasn't filled with all-consuming love anymore. It was blanked out, just as it had often been before this idyllic voyage.

Before he was able to say anything more, his phone started buzzing. He looked down at the number before sighing. "I have to get this."

After he'd been on the phone a minute, he turned to her. "I need to take care of something. It might take a while."

And with that he walked into another room. Savvy sat there for about ten minutes before a tear fell. She wiped it away and stood up, then gathered her purse before walking out of his suite.

If he wanted to find her, he would know where to look.

But Savvy slept restlessly for the rest of the night, if she slept at all, and Ashton never showed up to claim her. She'd given her heart to him, all of it, but maybe he now considered her not woman enough to keep her man. Or to take him. Whatever. That thought made her cry herself to sleep as the ship rocked back and forth on its journey home.

She did love him. Whether she wanted to or not, she loved him. And now he clearly thought that she wasn't good enough.

CHAPTER TWENTY-EIGHT

THREE DAYS WITH not much more than three words from Ashton.

Savvy tried to hide her despair. She tried telling herself that he was busy. After all, they'd been away from Seattle for ten days, and a lot had happened while they were out. But he was avoiding her. That was the reality she had to face. Nothing irrational about it.

It was over, and he just didn't want to have another messy scene like the one he'd been put through with his former fiancée. Savannah saw her best move forward as quitting. She'd be doing a favor both to Ashton and to herself. This job wasn't going to last a lot longer, and there was no way she was going to get to dive for sunken treasure now, so what was the point of hanging around?

Minor problem. If she left, she'd have no place to live for the rest of her summer, and she'd be giving up her final couple of paychecks. She hadn't taken the job here for the fun of it. And though she could probably find employment working in a café, that still didn't help with her housing situation.

So even though seeing the man she was in love with kept plunging jagged knives into her hurting heart and twisting them, she had to suck it up. At least that was something she was used to doing. She was also used to mixing metaphors.

The day was coming to an end, and as Savvy put away her supplies, she didn't think anything of the commotion down on the dock. Or she didn't think anything of it until she heard her name being called out.

"Savannah! Savannah! I see you down there."

Oh my gosh! She turned away but that did no good. The man continued to bellow and she was forced to look again.

"Don't try to pretend you don't know who I am! Tell these men to get their freaking hands off me!"

It was like she was in a horror show. Savvy was sickened to see the one person from her past whom she never, ever wanted to see again — her father, who was currently being restrained by two of the crewmen as they tried to escort him off the docks. He must have followed someone through the gate and bypassed the usual security.

How in the world had he traced her?

Something in her compelled her to come up closer during all the drama. "What are you doing here?" she had to ask.

She was within five feet of him when she smelled the cheap whiskey wafting off of him in waves. He didn't care if he risked his life and the lives of others by driving drunk. She'd forgotten how much she hated this man. Or maybe she hadn't.

"I came to see my daughter," he spluttered and slurred. "Are you going to tell these men to unhand me?"

"I just don't understand how you found me," she said slowly.

"You left your emergency contact information with the people taking care of your mother. And I'm your papa. I shouldn't have to try to track you down."

"Don't call yourself that. You're no father. In what universe do you think you've deserved the right to call yourself a father?"

The men holding her father didn't release their hold on him. She was more than grateful to them for that, though she was mortified that her co-workers were witnessing such an embarrassing moment in her life.

"I'm responsible for you being alive," he shouted at her. "You owe me, girlie. Both you and that worthless sister of yours. You just took off and left me all on my own after everything I did for you. Well, I need some help, and you're damn well going to give it to me."

She gazed into his bloodshot eyes. Was it no wonder she was a mess? With her mother in a mental facility and her father a raging alcoholic, she was surprised she'd made it this far in life. No. She wouldn't think that way. She was better than that, and she'd already proved it.

"Alexa and I are alive *in spite of you*. You abused us both, and you know it. You seemed to think that it was okay to talk with your fists. Our mother didn't stop you, and you literally drove the woman crazy. I stayed too long because I had to protect Alexa, but we're both grown up now, and we won't ever let you touch us again."

His eyes filled with rage and suddenly he broke free and made a charge for her. But though fears from a life full of them were almost choking her, Savvy refused to run from this man anymore. She raised her arm to block him, but he was able to slam his fist against her jaw. Stars exploded behind her eyes.

She stumbled backward and braced for the next impact, but as her vision cleared, she found her father flat on his back, knocked out cold. Ashton was standing there looking more frightening than she thought possible.

But the expression in his eyes changed in an instant. "Savvy, are you okay?" he asked as he stepped toward her.

She heard him speaking but she couldn't fully comprehend what was going on around her. Her head seemed to be buzzing still. Dang, the bastard who called himself her father had really landed a good hit to the side of her head.

"Savvy, can you speak?" Ashton asked her.

This finally motivated her into action. She stumbled away from him.

"I'm fine. I apologize for the embarrassment. I'll, um, take care of it," she said. But she hadn't the least idea how she was going to manage that.

"Nothing needs to be taken care of, Savvy. I want to know if you're okay."

"I'm fine," she said harshly as she backed away yet another step. She couldn't handle having him touch her. She knew that any contact of that kind would make her fall apart.

Sirens sounded in the distance, and she looked up the docks toward the road. The gates had been opened, and two police cars screeched to a stop inside. The men in blue jumped out and came racing down.

Savvy stood by silently as co-workers who'd witnessed the assault explained everything. And then the cops were asking her questions. Did she know who this was? Did she know where he lived? Why would he want to hurt her?

She couldn't even recognize her voice as she answered those questions. Her father regained consciousness as they were handcuffing him, and he struggled with them as they dragged him away. When they reached the top of the docks, he managed to head-butt one of the cops, causing the man to lose his footing and hit the ground.

The cop's partner drew out his Taser, and her father fell down writhing in pain. The man who had raised her — if what he'd done could be called that — was most likely going to prison for quite some time.

And Savvy felt absolutely nothing. Or very little, anyway.

That feeling of blankness was almost a blessing. No, it *was* a blessing. She would so much rather be numb than to deal with the horrible emotions of pain and sorrow. Numb she could handle. Numb she was used to.

And then people were walking away. The show had ended. And soon only she and Ashton were standing there, and even the light was beginning to fade in the sky.

Somehow she found herself much too close to her former lover, her *only* lover, as he reached out for her once again.

"Savvy, please let me help you."

And she snapped.

"Don't, Ashton! Don't pretend you care. You haven't spoken to me in three bloody days. Okay, maybe you managed to say hello." All her fear and pain rose to the surface like a fast-erupting volcano.

"Savvy, I'm sorry. I've just needed time to think," he said, and he stretched out his arms to her again.

"I swear, Mr. Storm, that if you touch me, I'm going to go psycho," she almost yelled as she backed further away. "Do you have a Taser on you? You might need it."

"I'm sorry you went through that. Please, tell me what I can do."

"I don't need or want your help, Ashton. I've done just fine on my own for a long time, and I will continue to do just fine. So stay the … heck away from me."

Savvy turned and walked off with her head held high. Neither her father nor Ashton would be able to break her. She was strong — no matter what the men in her life told her.

She had survived so much. And she would keep on surviving no matter what the fates threw at her next.

CHAPTER TWENTY-NINE

ASHTON REALLY WANTED to throw a drink back, but he decided that was probably the worst thing he could do at the moment. He was in his office, pacing like a madman, and Savvy was on her way in to see him. That was happening only because he'd pulled the boss card to get her there. He hated that it had to be this way.

He hadn't slept more than a couple of hours the night before. He was worried about this woman, a woman who had become so important to him. But she'd thrown him for a loop on the cruise, and he'd just needed time to figure out what to do.

Ashton had always known that he would need to bring heirs into this world. It was expected of him. He was a Storm, after all. And to add more fuel to that fire, he was also an Anderson. If he didn't produce heirs -— the best of the best — he wouldn't be doing his family duty.

But could he honestly give up a woman as amazing as Savvy just to produce children he wasn't even sure he wanted? That's what had been bothering him since they'd docked the cruise ship.

Add to that the traumatizing visit of Savvy's father the night before and he couldn't hold off from speaking to her anymore. He had to make sure she was really okay. He had to see if he was truly able to let her go.

"I was instructed to see you here."

Ashton turned to find Savvy standing stiffly in the doorway. She obviously wasn't pleased about being there.

"We need to talk, Savvy," he said, and he gestured to her to come inside his office.

She didn't budge. "Is this about work, Mr. Storm?"

He'd never heard such dullness in her voice before. Had he been that cruel to a woman who had brought him so much joy?

"Yes … and no," he answered at last.

"I only want to speak about work," she said, her arms crossed.

"Savvy, this is ridiculous. You throw a bombshell at me, and I take some time to think about it, and now you're acting as if the last couple of months didn't even happen. How mature is that?" The irritation in his tone probably rang out loud and clear.

Her shoulders slumped just a bit, but her eyes flared up. He could see she was trying to decide whether to turn away or to hear him out. He hoped like hell she'd pick the latter.

"In case you've forgotten, Ashton, you were the one to walk away from me and then avoid the hell out of me all because I said I didn't want to be a mother. I'm sorry if that doesn't go along with your life plans, but I'm done with being made to feel that I'm a lesser person because of my choices. I won't wait around for you to decide if I'm good enough for you to screw."

"You think that's all I want from you?"

"Yes, pretty much."

His eyes narrowed even more. "If all I wanted to do was screw you, as you so vulgarly put it, then why in the hell would I care or not whether you want children?"

That seemed to stump her. Her eyes took on a haunted look and her arms dropped. Good. She needed to mull over why the fact that she didn't want babies would make him reconsider their relationship. It was because he wasn't just thinking about today or tomorrow, but about ten years down the road. He was thinking of forever with her. Forever if they could be a real family.

"I care about you, Savvy. I care about you more than I thought it was possible to care about another person," he said when she didn't speak after several tense moments.

"That's ... that's impossible," she said, and she looked as if she were ready to tuck tail and run.

He wasn't allowing that. He strode forward and grabbed her arm, pulling her into the office. Once the two of them were at his desk, he leaned against it and slung his arms around her, trapping her against him.

"Yes, it's not only possible, but true. I care about you enough, my sweet Savannah, to change my own goals in life."

She was breathing heavily as she looked up at him. He could see she was trying to determine whether she could believe him or not.

"Ashton, this is insane. We barely know each other. It's just a fling. Or it was."

"Are you trying to convince me of that, Savvy, or convince yourself?"

She stood stiffly against him, but he rubbed his hands along her back and felt immense pride when she began to relax.

"I don't care if you want to admit it or not, Savvy. Okay, I do care. And you have to admit that you care about me, too. What we have is special, and I'm not willing or able to give you up. And I don't think you can walk away from me." He leaned closer, his lips only a breath away from hers.

"But ... the problems," she said.

He noticed she didn't actually use the word *children* in her stilted sentence.

"We can just be together right now, and the rest we'll figure out," he told her.

Tears sprang to her eyes and they filled with hope. It was all he needed to see. He barely had to move to connect their lips, and instant fire and comfort filled him when she reached up for him. She'd missed him as much as he'd missed her.

They truly were meant to be together.

"Would you mind taking your sleazy little hands off my future husband?"

The room went deathly silent as Ashton looked up to find Kalli in his doorway, and she was holding something between two of her well-manicured fingers. He was too stunned and then too pissed to be able to utter a single word.

"Haven't we been here before, darling?" Kalli said. "You with your hands on the cleaning staff while I'm standing like a fool in the doorway? Have you grown addicted to the smell of bleach?"

Ashton found his voice at last. "What are you doing here, Kallista? I'm not in the mood to deal with you right now."

"Of course you aren't, darling. Not when you have your tongue halfway down this slut's throat," the woman said. "Haven't you learned by now not to fraternize with the hired help? They have no manners and they don't know how to behave in society. It's a recipe for embarrassment. I guess we all have to dabble in lukewarm water once in a while, though, just to get it out of our system." She moved a short way toward the two of them.

"Get the hell out of my office," Ashton growled. Savvy, who wasn't saying a word, pulled away from his arms, making him even angrier. How had he ever thought to marry the "high-class" bitch who was now invading their privacy? He took a determined step toward his ex-fiancée.

"Be careful, darling," Kalli said. "You wouldn't want to upset me too terribly. It might harm our child."

He stopped moving; she took what she was holding and waved it high in the air. Savvy gasped from behind him, and he realized that what Kalli was brandishing must have some sort of significance. He took a good long look.

"Is that an ultrasound?" he asked, and he suddenly grew weak at the knees.

"It certainly is, my love. I knew you'd want proof I was carrying."

And then Kalli was placing that photograph into his hands. But he couldn't focus on the image in front of him, not for the life of him. Or for the life of …

"Here, let me point out the little head," Kalli told him a little too smugly. Then he heard words but not full sentences from this woman, the blue-blood hussy who had managed to get his ring on her finger before he'd wised up.

"… healthy pregnancy … low blood pressure … ten weeks along …"

There was so much buzzing in his ears that he could barely process what she was saying to him.

"How?" He hadn't slept with her in … crap! In about ten weeks.

"If I need to explain the birds and the bees to you, Ashton, you couldn't have been very active with your little low-class floozy for the past couple of months."

Some of the buzzing started to end. "The baby can't be mine," he insisted.

Kalli's face fell, and Ashton doubted himself. Was this truly his child? The small amount of hope scared the shit out of him.

"Yes, Ashton, this child is yours. But if you don't want it, I'll go ahead and terminate the pregnancy," she said as she turned and began walking from the room. She made it back to the door before he found himself yelling.

"No! If that child is mine, I have a say in this," he absolutely bellowed.

"I'm not having the child if I'm not married to the father. So make your decision, and make it fast," she snapped. And then she sashayed away. But not before shooting a death glare at Savvy.

Ashton stumbled backward and sank down into his chair before he looked up to see Savvy shivering in the corner. She appeared to be in shock.

"I'm so sorry, Savvy, so very sorry," he said.

"It's okay, Ashton. I understand," she finally replied, her voice so small.

"I can't abandon my child." That was his best attempt to explain.

"I know."

And Savvy walked out of his life almost as quickly as she'd walked into it.

CHAPTER THIRTY

"WHO IS THE best sister in all the land?"

Savannah looked up, her expression not changing even a bit as Alexa rushed into the room, a grin on her face and a piece of paper in her hand. The paper-in-the-hand thing nearly sent Savvy into tears all over again, but she hadn't cried in a week, and she wasn't about to start again.

She didn't honestly understand how a person could cry non-stop for two weeks straight. She had to have no tears left in her system. She also didn't understand why in the world she had been crying at all. It wasn't like she was a drama queen, or a woman who threw fits — not ever.

She blamed her excess of emotion on the loss of her job. She hadn't even thought twice about quitting once Kalli had walked back into Ashton's life with the one thing she was willing to give him that Savvy wasn't. At least Alexa had taken her in, even if the place to stay was a very uncomfortable secondhand couch in the world's smallest apartment.

"You're the best sister," Savannah said, doing her best to smile.

"Of course I am. Because I got something for you that is going to get you off my couch for at least the afternoon," Alexa said, waving the piece of paper around. "Then I will probably have to burn the stupid couch 'cause I don't think you've moved from that exact same spot for the past three weeks," she muttered.

"I heard that, Lexie."

"Ah, my sweet big sister, I wasn't trying to be quiet," Alexa said with another hop.

After her sister placed the bit of paper in her hands, Savannah tried to figure out what she was looking at. When it finally hit her, an actual smile almost lifted up her lips.

"How could you afford this, Lexie?"

"Don't worry about the how and just go jump in the shower and get dressed, and then get the heck out of here for the next twelve hours or so," Alexa said, tugging on Savvy's hand.

"It's for today?"

"Yep, and it's a one-time deal, so hurry, hurry, hurry," Alexa said, now pushing against Savvy's back to thrust her into the bathroom.

"My clothes," Savannah called out.

"I'm getting them. You shower; I'll play servant."

"Are you trying to get rid of me for a particular reason?" Savvy asked through the closed door as she stripped off her pajamas.

"Not at all," Alexa called back, but Savannah knew only too well when her sister was playing fast and loose with the truth.

"I'm so excited about this, Alexa, that I think I'm going to let you get away with lying to me."

Then the conversation stopped as Savvy turned on the water and did her best to send her worries down the drain. So what if she'd fallen in love with the wrong man? Didn't all women have to do that at least once in their life? Of course they did. Even if she was supersmart — and she probably was, if she said so herself — it didn't mean she never made any mistakes.

Before she knew it she was singing, very off tune, *"I'm gonna wash that man right out of my hair..."* If only it were that easy. At least her sister wasn't shouting at her through the doorway. Not that yelling at her would stop her mad singing tirade. Savvy decided she might just be going a little bit crazy. Didn't they say love made a person crazy? She'd been smart not to go through the teenage angst of love. At least she was now a bit wiser and though it was killing her a little bit more and more inside, she knew she would survive this, but as an impressionable teen, she might not have been strong enough.

An hour later, Savannah found herself driving to the ferry, which took her to a dock that wasn't far from Ashton's place of business.

That made her a little antsy, but when she looked around, she didn't spot the man, so she figured this was just a coincidence. It had to be. Her sister wouldn't sell her out. No way.

"Savvy, it's so good to see you again."

Jumping at the booming voice of Joseph Anderson, Savvy turned around too quickly and stumbled to her knees, instantly sending a shooting flash of pain through her kneecap. Tears sprang to her eyes, but she wasn't sure if it was from embarrassment or pain — embarrassment was more likely.

"I'm so sorry, darling," Joseph Anderson exclaimed as he instantly bent down and helped her to her feet. His two brothers were right there with him, both looking equally concerned.

"Please don't apologize. I'm such a klutz," she said, trying to get the tears out of her eyes. Dang it!

"I've been told I'm too loud and startle people," Joseph said sheepishly.

"No, really. It's so nice to see you again, Joseph," she told him, hoping he would just drop the subject.

He gave her an assessing look and then smiled big before grabbing her up for a monster-sized bear hug. Her breath rushed from her.

"It's wonderful to see you both as well, Richard and George," she added, almost afraid of what would follow.

Those hugs weren't quite so bone-crushing, though.

"What are you three up to?" she asked as she looked out at the nice boat sitting at the dock with no sign of a dive instructor.

"We ran into your sister at the hospital when we were attending a board meeting," Richard said, "and she was telling us how disappointed you were that you hadn't gotten to go on a dive this summer."

"So we arranged one for you," George piped in.

Savannah looked around in panic. She just couldn't see Ashton again. Her heart was just now starting to heal, sort of, and spending the day with that man would undo her limited progress.

"My nephew Austin has a lot of diving experience," Joseph told her. "It was something of a hobby for him for a lot of years. He and his cousin Lance will be here any minute now."

She let out the breath she'd been holding. "You really didn't need to do this for me," she said with a smile that kept growing wider. "But I do appreciate it. I should tell you to go about your day, but I'm eager to get into some scuba gear."

"This is no trouble at all for any of us," George said. "It's a beautiful Saturday with calm waters. And Austin happens to know of a place where there's a wreck that hasn't been completely picked through."

Savannah's eyes lit up as she looked toward the boat.

"Sorry we're late. Got caught in traffic," a man said as he approached. He had a bit of gray at his temples, but he was still devastatingly handsome, as were all the Storm and Anderson men she'd met.

"Yes, if Austin didn't drive like an eighty-year-old blind grandma, we would have made it here an hour ago." This came from Lance, whom Savvy had met at Joseph's party and that one time on the docks, a little earlier, when she'd been with her sister. Lance was a definite flirt. And it had been more than obvious that the man had found her sister attractive. Savvy wasn't so sure about her sister's feelings.

"Shut up, Lance," the first man said. "I'm Austin. And I'm only a few years older than this cousin of mine, whose driving is much worse than mine. Of course, we did meet briefly at my uncle's bonfire."

How in the world could she have forgotten this man? Maybe because she'd been so completely consumed by the fire in her blood that was Ashton.

"I'm truly grateful that you're taking me out. I haven't been able to dive for over six months now, and I'm pumped up about it," she said, taking Austin's hand and then Lance's.

"Well, then," Lance said, "we'd better get this show on the waves."

"Are you three joining us?" Savannah asked the infamous meddlers.

"Not this trip, sweetheart. We have business to take care of," Joseph boomed.

She was disappointed to hear that. She really enjoyed the company of the dynamic older men. They weren't aging gracefully at all and they didn't seem to give a damn. She only hoped she had half their energy as the years continued to pass.

She barely had time to register what was going on before she was being led to the boat, and then they were casting off. So once again she was on the sea, but this was for a day trip only. Maybe that was a good thing. She didn't need any more storms in her life — either the thundering ones or the ones who had it as a surname. And who could also be terrifying forces of nature in their own way.

"Which wreck site are we going to?" she asked as they cruised along.

"Well, we aren't quite sure," Lance said, "but we think we might have made a new discovery."

Savannah's heart instantly began to pound.

"What ship do you think it is?" she asked, now in more of a hurry to get to the site.

"We've only been out here twice, and it's not listed on the registry of known wrecks," Austin told her.

"So which ship do you think it might be?" She really wasn't into the suspense.

"It could be the schooner *Anna C. Anderson*," Lance finally said.

"Really?" she gasped.

"Could be," Austin told her, stressing two of his cousin's words.

"Oh my, that ship departed from Oysterville on Shoalwater Bay with cargo and fresh oysters on its way to San Francisco in 1869. It disappeared with seven people on board."

"How in the world do you know that off the top of your head?" Lance asked her.

"I've studied all the wrecks and lost ships of the West Coast. I've studied other regions too, but this area is the most accessible for me. If it's truly the schooner, you'll be named as the ones to find it," she said with delight. "And knowing I was here early on in that discovery would be just amazing."

"If you can identify it, then you'll get all the credit," Lance replied.

Tears instantly popped into Savvy's eyes and she had to turn away from the two men. "I'm not the one who found it," she reminded them.

Lance tried to reassure her. "It doesn't mean nearly as much to either of us."

After about an hour spent zooming along, the men chatting nonstop, Austin and Lance secured the boat, and soon Savvy was in the diving gear that they'd provided. She couldn't help but feel elated as the three of them jumped into the water.

The sea was full of mysteries, some of them fascinating, some terrifying, and some downright awe-inspiring. But as they sank farther and farther below the surface of the ocean, she began to see pieces of what might be a boat.

Time and the harshness of the sea had torn it apart, but close investigation allowed her to determine that it was definitely a shipwreck. To identify which one it was, however, would take more than an afternoon. Hell, even after months of study, she still might never identify it.

But Savvy wasn't going to let that thought keep her from trying. She would come out as often as time and her limited funds would allow. She managed to turn up a few treasures among the wreckage, but nothing of monetary value. That didn't matter at all. She wasn't seeking riches — she was seeking *treasure*.

When Austin indicated it was time to go up, she looked at her oxygen and realized how low it was. She usually kept a better eye on that, but she was so happy to float along the bottom of the sea, particularly now, when everything else in her life wasn't going swimmingly. True, the diving site wasn't too far off one of the small islands scattered along the West Coast, but it still felt as if she were in the middle of thousands of miles of ocean.

When her head popped above the water, she removed her mouthpiece and sent a grin in Austin's direction. There was so much she wanted to discuss. But just at that moment she noticed another boat anchored right by the one they'd brought out.

And her smile vanished.

She knew that boat, knew exactly who it belonged to.

Swimming back over to Austin's boat, she pulled herself up the ladder — and came face to face with Ashton. He was wearing diving gear, and it was wet, but she hadn't seen him down in the deep water. She'd been in her own world, and maybe she had seen him but just thought it was Lance or Austin. But it didn't matter. She wasn't letting the sight of him ruin her wonderful day.

"Did you have a good time, Savvy?" he asked.

What the hell? He was acting as if there weren't a whole lot of misery between the two of them. Or misery on her part — he'd probably felt none.

"What are you doing here, Ashton? I wasn't under the impression that you were invited." She was surprised by how cool she was able to sound just then.

But he seemed unaffected. "My father told me that my brother and cousin were out diving in our spot. I thought I'd join them."

"Your spot?" she asked.

"Yes, we found it together," he told her.

"Oh."

She was completely deflated. Now, even if she did prove it was the *Anna C Anderson*, it wasn't just Austin and Lance's right to give her the credit. And she didn't want to go diving in a place where Ashton could show up any time he wanted.

"Why so bummed out? It looks like you found a thing or two," he said, reaching toward her.

She quickly backed away. "Don't touch me, Ashton," she grated out. "Please." She hated that she was so very close to breaking down.

"Savvy ... I ... I've missed you," he finally said, and she nearly collapsed at his feet.

But she didn't. "You don't have the right to miss me, Ashton. You're going to be a father. Our entire relationship has been wrong — right from the beginning. You were engaged to be married, and still I let you pursue me. But now you're going to have a baby with her. I can't be with you," she told him, hating the choked feeling in her throat.

"I just miss you, Savvy."

"It doesn't matter, Ashton. None of it does."

Lance and Austin were now climbing onto the boat, and she was glad.

"I found something down there," Ashton told her.

"I'm happy for you," Savannah said.

"I want you to have it."

He held something out, but she couldn't see what it was. She didn't want to even look, though, because she couldn't and wouldn't accept it.

"Thank you, but no. Give it to Kalli, whatever it is."

"Kalli wouldn't appreciate it. This was made for you," he said and he put it into her hand.

Though time and circumstances hadn't been good to this little piece of jewelry, it could easily be cleaned up, and it would be back to its former beauty. It was a necklace, an unusual piece that she was guessing was silver, but it could be gold as well. They wouldn't know until it was cleaned. It was a heart with a curious pattern swirling up to circle a light blue stone. It was simple — and beautiful. And she desperately wanted to keep it.

"No. You take it," she said. "Please go back to your boat and let me go home." Savvy thrust the necklace back into his hand.

Ashton walked away from her, just as she'd asked him to do. He chatted with his brother and cousin for a few minutes and then returned to his boat. He rode off before they did.

Savvy knew that this would be the last time she would see him. She sat in the back of Austin's boat and was thankful that he and Lance left her alone as she slumped over the side and let her tears fall into the sea. And she'd thought that she was cried out.

It was fitting to have said her final goodbye this way — at sea — to the man she loved so much. When she returned to the shore, she would leave it all behind. She had no other choice.

Later that night, as Savvy was stretched out on the couch with a thriller book in her hand about a woman seeking revenge on the man who had done her wrong, she heard a knock on the apartment door. Alexa was gone, leaving her no choice but to see who it was.

"Delivery for Savanna Mills," the man announced through the door in a loud voice.

She looked through the peephole and he seemed to be legit. So she opened the door and he handed over a package after having her sign her name.

It took her a while but she looked over the simple box and actually opened it. And she wished she hadn't.

Inside, on a bed of velvet, was the necklace Ashton had found. It was silver, a beautiful, simple silver locket, most likely belonging to a fisherman's wife. Next to it was a note:

The aquamarine in the center of this locket symbolizes courage, loyalty, honesty, and beauty. Aquamarines are also considered sacred to Neptune, the Roman god of the sea. Wear this and you will always have a safe voyage. When I found this, I knew that it could belong only to you.

CHAPTER THIRTY-ONE

ASHTON HAD THROWN away the best thing that had ever happened to him, and he had done it for nothing. Honor meant zip to some people. What a freaking fool he was.

"I told you two months ago to get the hell out of my life! I meant it then and I still mean it now."

"But, baby ... we can work this out," Kalli cried.

"I love that you can say the word *baby*, Kallista. How can any human being be so despicable as to fake a pregnancy?"

Kalli looked at him with wide eyes. "I just knew we needed more time."

"Don't try to sway me with the equally fake tears — you'd probably use the word *faux* anyway. I wasn't kidding, Kalli. Get out of here now or I swear you won't like what happens next."

Her back straightened and her tears dried up. "What are you going to do, Ashton? Hit me?"

"Oh, no, dear, Kalli. Even if I don't consider you a real woman, I would never hit a … female." He wouldn't call her a lady. "I'll hit you where it counts — in the media."

He had nothing to lose anymore. He would tell all to the reporters who loved gossip, and every one of them did. He didn't give a damn if it put him in a bad light too. He'd lost the woman he loved, so what the hell did any of it matter? It didn't.

"Your money isn't worth this, Ashton."

"There it is," he said with the first smile he'd felt on his lips in months.

"Yeah, so what? That stupid little trollop you were with won't get her hands on it either now," she said, and her laugh sounded as if it were coming from a mad scientist. Or maybe from Mr. Hyde.

Damn, he'd been a fool to think he could marry for a pedigree instead of love. When the true colors came out, they really came out.

He picked up the phone and started punching in numbers. He was done.

"I'm going!" she said, and she ran out the door. He knew he wouldn't see her again. It was over.

Ashton ended the call before it had ever started ringing. He didn't want to waste another thought on such a greedy, worthless human being.

One who'd cost him everything that had any real value in life.

Ashton hung his head in sorrow. He'd tried getting ahold of Savvy, but she wasn't enrolled at her university anymore. Had she given up on her degree? Her sister wouldn't tell him where she was, and his whole life seemed to be lost now. And it was all because he'd felt he had to do the right thing.

But it had been three months since he'd last seen Savvy on Austin's boat in the Pacific. She was gone. It was time for him to get on with his life.

No, Ashton didn't want to face the world, but he couldn't keep hiding away. He had a business to run and a family he loved, even though they'd recently been driving him crazy. Every single one of them seemed to be asking him at least once a week whether he'd seen Savvy. If not several times a week.

And yet he couldn't help but gaze out the massive windows of his secluded house and wonder what Savvy was doing. Who she was with. Had she moved on? He could most likely get these answers with a little effort, but she'd made it more than clear that their relationship was over and done with, kaput, *fini*.

A small voice tried to tell him that the obstacle was no longer in their way. But he'd chosen to go back to Kalli, and he'd broken Savvy's heart. She wouldn't forgive him for that. And she shouldn't.

It didn't help, though, to know how much his father loved Savvy, how much his uncles, siblings, and cousins loved her too. From the moment he'd informed them that he was engaged to Kalli again, and told them why he'd made that choice, they hadn't believed her story.

Their doubts had pushed Ashton to demand further testing — that hadn't been easy — and it had proved that the woman had made the entire thing up. She wasn't pregnant and she'd never been pregnant. She'd probably been planning to fake a miscarriage after she'd dragged him down the aisle. He had no idea how she'd managed to get an ultrasound photo.

But where there was a will, there was a way — especially when billions were involved. Kallista Blanche Huntington-Hart had destroyed his life. Not bad for a scheming bitch. Okay, so he had to take some responsibility here for taking himself down.

The clanging of the phone nearly made Ashton jump out of his skin. That was almost funny, and if he could have still found enjoyment in life, he might have done so then.

"Where have you been?"

His father wasn't normally a man to yell, but Ashton had to yank the phone away to save his eardrum.

"I've been busy, Father. And how are you?"

"I've been worried about you — that's how I am," Richard told him.

"I'm sorry I've caused you any stress. I'm doing just fine."

"That's good, I suppose," Richard said before letting out a long sigh on the other end of the line.

"What do you want to tell me, Dad?" The last thing Ashton wanted was to draw this out.

"Well, I don't think I should gossip, or anything …"

Ashton knew instantly that his father was enjoying himself, but he also knew that he had to play along with the game if he wanted to get any information. And now the old man had made him curious.

"We both know that you're going to tell me whatever it is, so just spit it out," he said, his lips almost lifting.

"Well, it's just that I ran into Savvy the other day …"

Ashton immediately sat up straight in his chair.

"You did? Where was she? How is she?" he blurted out.

"She seemed … good. Really good, actually," Richard said quietly.

"Oh … that's great," Ashton replied. He was lying, of course. He didn't find it so great that Savvy had moved on so easily while he was still pining away for her.

"Yeah, she was with some guy," Richard said. "I think he's a banker. Something like that."

Ashton's eyes turned into slits, but his voice was deceptively calm. "She's seeing another man?"

"Well, you sure as hell aren't courting her. You don't expect such an amazing woman as her to remain single for long. Do you, son?"

Ashton could almost feel his dad's disappointed eye roll through the phone. "Where is she living?" he asked between his teeth.

"She's apparently living with the fellow in a house out in Snoqualmie. It's a real nice place."

"She moved in with this white-collar guy?" Ashton thundered.

"I knew I shouldn't have told you," Richard grumbled.

"What's the address?" Ashton said. His voice had grown quieter and quieter with each word.

"It's probably wrong to give it to you. I don't want you doing something stupid. Not that being stupid is your style. Or is it now?"

Ashton had a hard time not throwing his phone through one of the picture windows he'd just been staring through.

"Just give me the damn address, Dad."

The other end of the line went totally silent, and Ashton had to count to about a hundred in his head before he said something else that he shouldn't.

Richard finally spoke. "I don't appreciate hearing you speak to me in that churlish way, Ashton."

"I'm sorry. You're absolutely right that I shouldn't talk to you that way. It's just that I have something of Savvy's that I need to return to her and I have a busy week. If I get that out of the way, I can get back to work," the boy lied. He'd really pulled that out of his ass, in fact.

"Oh, in that case, son, here you go."

Richard rattled off the address, and Ashton nearly broke his pen as he scribbled it down, because he was pressing so hard.

And when he hung up the phone, Ash had to sit there a minute longer before he moved. In the mood he was in, he was afraid he was indeed going to do something stupid. Just as he had that thought, a bitter laugh escaped his throat. Of course he was going to do something stupid. *Stupidity* was very likely another one of his unfortunate middle names — his father had said as much. The story of his life.

He was in love with a woman who had obviously moved on, and he didn't take too kindly to being replaced. Maybe it was time that he reminded Savvy of just how good the two of them had been together. He could move on as well — right back to her.

With this thought, he rose and went straight to his car. He was glad the drive took him over an hour. This was one of the reasons he worked on the docks in the San Juan Islands. He hated Seattle traffic.

As rain began drizzling down, he found the address his father had given him, parked across the street, and looked at the house.

Once again, this whole situation stumped him. What in the hell was he doing? What was he going to say?

Maybe this hadn't been his best idea ever.

The heavy clouds were turning the morning sky dark when the front door opened and a man stepped out. Savvy was holding the door, laughing at something the man said, and Ashton's gut clenched. In her gigantic robe, slippers on her feet, and her hair in a sloppy bun, she was still the most beautiful sight he'd ever been blessed with.

The banker, or whatever he was, turned around and bent down, kissed her cheek, and then jumped into his car and drove off while Savvy proceeded down the driveway to gather the morning paper. Ashton was a mass of jealous rage.

Before Savvy could get back inside the house, Ashton climbed out of his own car and, without realizing the force he was using, slammed the door loud enough to be heard by everyone in the vicinity.

She jumped. When she looked across the street, their eyes met. His narrowed; hers widened. Screw all his hesitating. He took long strides toward her and he was sure that his scowl turned even more vicious as she bounded toward her front door.

But his temper blew right on through the roof when she masked her expression into polite boredom — as if she were dealing with a pesky neighbor.

"Hi, Ashton. You're a long ways from home." Nothing in her tone showed him how she felt about his impromptu visit.

"It's cold out here. Invite me inside," he told her as he put his hand on the door, ensuring she wouldn't be able to slam it in his face.

"I'm actually not feeling all that well and I was getting ready to lie back down," she said as she hugged her robe to her just a little bit tighter.

Dream on, sweetheart. Ashton wasn't going away that easily. He stepped forward, and her pupils dilated, this time as if she was afraid. That made him even angrier. He'd never hurt her, and he was furious that she would think — for even a second — that he would. No matter how upset he was, he couldn't hurt her.

Well, he would never hurt her physically. The emotional damage he'd inflicted on her had been plenty. But he didn't want to be that monster. He wanted to be her hero.

"I'm sure you can make time for an old … let's just say *friend*," he told her. Then he walked right past her into the house.

He heard her heavy sigh as she was left with no other choice but to shut the door or continue letting the cold air inside.

When he turned back around to look at her, his gut clenched. Damn, he had missed this woman, missed her more than he could have ever comprehended. He missed the way she made him laugh, the way she was insatiable in his bed, the way her hand would play with the silken strands of her hair when she was nervous. He just missed — her.

And he was determined to have her back.

CHAPTER THIRTY-TWO

SAVANNAH WAS TRYING desperately to control her breathing, trying to make sure Ashton couldn't see from her face or her body language how tough this meeting was on her. She was also trying to keep other things hidden from him, and it was taking a lot out of her to do all of this at once.

The last few months had been horrible for her, and she was only now beginning to be able to function. Seeing him again like this was going to set her back in a big way.

"Can you make this quick, Ashton? I really am tired." She walked past him with her chin up, and he followed her to the living room. She didn't take off her robe, but she sat down on the couch, curling her legs beneath her.

"It's the morning. Why are you so tired?" he asked.

She glared at him. "That's none of your business, Ashton."

He leaned against the wall. "What have you been doing lately, Savvy? I looked for you at your university, and I discovered that you were no longer enrolled."

Dang, why did the man have to be so handsome, even wearing that scowl of his and doing his intimidation thing? She hated that she was still attracted to him even after everything that had happened. She hated even more how much her heart hurt to be in the same room with him and how she didn't have the right to run her fingers through his hair or lay her head on his chest while he comforted her.

"What do you mean?" she finally said when she realized he'd asked her a question.

"I'll put this another way, Savannah. Why aren't you in graduate school?" He then looked toward her front door.

What was he looking for?

"I needed to take a couple of terms off," she told him.

"Why's that?"

"I ... uh ... well ..." She felt as if she were being interrogated and she didn't like the feeling. Did he know? Was he just toying with her? She squirmed uncomfortably on the couch. She was starting to feel her stomach roll and she was desperate to end this conversation.

"You need to go now, Ashton. I don't want to try to be friends with you," she told him, angry that she felt close to tears. That anger is what saved her from releasing them.

"Why can't we be friends, Savvy? Are you worried your roommate won't like it?" he snarled.

"Why would I be worried about that?"

"Really? You have no idea what I'm talking about? I saw the guy walk out of here, Savvy. I saw the kiss," he shouted, coming closer.

"So what? Why are you raising your voice like this?" *What the heck was going on?*

"Because I don't like that you jumped from my bed into some other guy's," he said, his body tense as he looked down at her.

"Ashton, this isn't what it looks like, but even if it were, it's not your concern, and you know it." She stopped speaking when she saw his eyes flash.

"Dammit, Savvy. I love you, okay? I love you so much I hurt from it. I can't think of anyone else but you. I can't stand the thought of you with another man, of him touching you, laughing with you, taking care of you. It makes me want to smash my fists into the wall. I just … I screwed up. I know I did. But I know you love me too, and we're meant to be together. Don't let stupid mistakes keep us apart."

Though those words meant everything to her, they also meant nothing. He was only there out of jealousy, obviously because he believed she was in a new relationship. He was still engaged to Kalli, and he still wasn't hers. He could never be hers.

"Ashton, Jim is my roommate — that's all. We aren't lovers; we aren't boyfriend and girlfriend. He was looking for a roommate and I applied. We've become close …," she began to say, but she stopped herself. She didn't want to tell Ashton the reason they were close.

"That's how it begins, Savvy. You get close and then you get closer," he growled.

"He's gay, Ashton. We're about as close as we're going to get," she told him with a sad smile.

"Oh," he said, the breath whooshing out of his mouth. "Hmmm … Have you seen my father lately?" The change in topic stumped her for a moment.

"Yes, a few days ago. Jim's a lawyer and is working on something for your father, I think. I was at the office dropping something off for Jim when Richard walked in."

She stopped. Oh, she should have known Richard would immediately go to his son and tell him where she was. Dang it. She should have made him promise not to do that. He wouldn't go against his word — he was a man of honor. Had he set up this whole roommate business for some ulterior motive? She'd been wearing a thick coat, her body not exposed. Richard couldn't have known her secret … Now her head was spinning trying to figure out if he had somehow known.

"Good old Dad," Ashton said, coming to the same conclusion as she had.

But then he stepped toward her again and she didn't know what to think. The look in his eyes almost resembled love. But despite what he'd said a few minutes before, that couldn't be.

"I'm sorry, Ashton. But this is all a big misunderstanding. You really should leave now."

He knelt in front of her on the couch and reached for her hand. Savvy's heart thudded and throbbed.

"Weren't you listening to me, Savvy? I love you. I need you. Please don't throw us away. Do I have to beg?" He lifted her hand up and kissed the back of it.

"But ... Kalli," she whimpered.

"I screwed up, Savvy. I thought I wanted a baby more than anything else. I thought I was supposed to continue the Storm line with the perfect children. Did you know that she lied about being pregnant?"

"What?"

"But even before I found out she'd lied, I knew I didn't want to be with her. No, I wouldn't abandon my child, but I couldn't marry a woman I didn't love and who didn't love me. I never slept with her again after she came back. I couldn't do that when I was in love with you. But she did lie. She was never pregnant and she's now out of my life forever."

"I ... I don't know what to say," she finally muttered.

"Say you forgive me. I was a fool. I want you, Savvy, only you. I don't need children. I don't need anything but you. And for you to love me. Please forgive me and then marry me. Let's be a family — just the two of us. That's all I need."

And Savvy could no longer hold the tears back. She needed to answer him, but she couldn't find the words.

Ashton sat down, pulled her legs over his, and caressed her cheeks with infinite fondness. "I've missed you so much, Savvy — so, so much. There hasn't been a day that's passed since I last saw you that I haven't thought about you, that I haven't sighed your name before falling asleep. I thought I could stay in a world without love, but I can't. You showed me a new way of life, and now that's all I want."

"Oh, Ashton, I … I love you too," she said with a sob as she took his hand in hers.

"Marry me, Savvy. Please be mine forever. It will always be just you and me."

"Well, that might be a little bit difficult," she said as she pulled his hand toward her and slipped it beneath her robe.

Ashton's eyes widened in shock, and then in wonder, and now she knew beyond a doubt that he'd had no idea she was carrying his child. She'd truly believed she hadn't wanted to be a mother, but knowing she was carrying the baby of the man she loved had changed the way she felt. Her bump was small, but it was definitely telling as she approached her fourth month.

"Yes, she's yours," Savvy whispered. "And, yes, I love her with all my heart."

He didn't speak for several moments as he stroked her thickening stomach, adoration and awe in his eyes and in his touch.

"I love you so much, Savvy," he told her. "Thank you for protecting our child when I wasn't here for you."

He then pulled her into his arms and kissed her until she lost her breath for all new reasons. When his lips finally released hers, she smiled as she looked into his eyes.

"Yes, Ashton Storm, I would be more than happy to become your wife."

"Let's go home, my love," he said before kissing her again.

Savvy's life could truly begin now that she had everything she hadn't even known she wanted.

EPILOGUE

THE BOAT SWAYED gently on the water as lightning flashed in the sky several miles away. The clouds were high and dark, but no rain dared to fall while Joseph and George Anderson and Richard Storm settled back in their deck chairs and enjoyed a nice scotch. A storm over the Pacific gave a good show when it didn't come *too* close.

"I have to admit I was worried there for a while," Joseph said. He wasn't worried anymore. And he wasn't talking about the weather.

"I know," Richard replied with a shake of his head. "I wasn't so sure that Ashton was going to take the bait, to go over the edge when he thought Savvy had found someone else. But I had to do everything in my power to get those kids back together."

"We're only helping them out. It isn't like we're doing anything wrong," George told his brothers.

"Of course we aren't doing anything wrong. We haven't had a miss yet, but those dang kids — none of them appreciate all we do for them, or the amount of time and effort that goes in to making sure they're happy," Joseph grumbled.

"Someday they'll see how much we've done for them," George replied. "Until that happens, whatever will be will be."

"Well, the best decision I could have ever made was moving to the West Coast," Richard said. "Not only have I gained two brothers — ones I seem to have known my whole life — but I have a slew of nieces and nephews to boot. And with all the babies popping up around here, we could start up our own town."

"I like that idea," Joseph boomed. "It could be Andersonville. Not the first town by that name, but one of the best."

"With a giant lake called Storm Pond," Richard said.

"I have to admit I wouldn't mind getting out of the hustle and bustle of the city," George told them. "I've really enjoyed spending time on these islands the last few years."

"Yes. The city was great in my working years," Joseph said, "but now it takes me so dang long to get anywhere in all this traffic."

"Don't forget that we have one of my children to go," Richard told the boys, "and then maybe we can spend a few months a year out in Montana with our good friends there."

George was clearly fascinated. "Hmm. That doesn't sound like such a bad idea. I know that our pal Martin Whitman is struggling to get his youngest two sons married off. If those young men are still single by the time Lance is putting a ring on some girl's finger, we might just have to head out there and give him some more help."

"There's nothing that says we can't do both at the same time," Richard told them.

"That's true," Joseph said. "We're crafty men, and great at what youngsters call multitasking. I think the goal this year will be to get both Lance and Martin's boys, Michael and Cam, married off."

"Ah, I wouldn't mind another wedding like the one we just had. Savvy looked absolutely breathtaking in her beaded ivory gown. Her blushing cheeks and those eyes so full of love brought tears to my eyes," said the bride's father-in-law.

"Yes, and in a couple of months more we get another baby added into the family." Joseph raised his glass in celebration and triumph.

"How many children does that make now?" George asked after clinking glasses.

Both Joseph and Richard sat back.

"Dang. That might take a minute for me to figure out," Richard finally said.

"Maybe if we're losing count," George replied, "we can say we've accomplished our goals."

Both of his brothers turned to George, and their look was suggestive — *was he insane?*

"You must be kidding. There could never be enough toddlers running through the halls of our houses. Because someday, you know, they are going to grow up, and then they'll need to find their own true loves," Joseph said with a sly smile.

"Your Jasmine sure has come into her own over the years. I can't believe she's fifteen years old already," George said with a sigh.

"Yes, Jasmine will always hold a special place in my heart as my first grandchild," Joseph told him. "Plus, she's just as sweet as her mama."

George now guffawed. "She's stubborn like her grandfather, you mean."

"A little stubbornness is good for a lady. It means the menfolk won't be able to treat her wrong," Joseph said.

"All right. Let's wait a few years to focus on Jasmine or any of the other grandkids," Richard told them. "Right now, it's time to set our eyes on Lance. We've been leaving him to his own devices for too long. It's time to find him a bride."

"I don't think we're going to have to look too far," Richard said with a laugh.

"Did we miss something?" George asked.

"I can't believe neither of you noticed him and Savvy's little sister sending each other some pretty heated looks at the wedding," Richard said with glee.

"Why in the world didn't you say something sooner?" Joseph demanded.

Richard smiled. "We've been busy."

"That's true," George said.

"So let's get started," Joseph told the men.

"Agreed," his brothers said, and they all leaned a little closer.

Heaven was right where they sat. They had a view of the crystal-clear water and the dark, thundering skies. And they could see in their mind's eye even more houses filled up all around them with love, laughter, and plans for tomorrow.

Continue reading for an excerpt from the first book in the Baby for the Billionaire Series:

The
Tycoon's
Revenge

Baby for the Billionaire: Book One

PROLOGUE

A STAR FELL FROM the heavens and Jasmine watched in awe as the light slowly dimmed, and then disappeared entirely.

The feel of Derek's hand stroking her back was pure bliss, and she felt as if she could lie here all night long, never return to the real world. This place they'd created together was perfect — no father telling her it was wrong, no worries, no troubles.

"I love you so much, Jasmine," Derek whispered in her ear. "You are my world, my life."

"You know how much I love you," she replied, lifting her head to accept the gentle kiss from his lips. Her body melted all over again at his slightest touch.

"I hate having to take you back home tonight," he said, pulling her even closer.

"Then don't," she begged.

"Your father would hunt us down," he told her.

"I don't care. I know what I want and that's to be with you, Derek."

"Then we should run away together. I've actually been thinking about it a lot, about moving on from here." As she flinched, he added, "Only with you, my love; I'd never leave you behind. Here's my idea. My dad will be fine. He's starting his new business. It's foolproof. He wants me to run it with him, but I have bigger dreams than running a computer store. I want to go to the city, intern for someone like Bill Gates, learn from them, and make something of myself," he said, passion flowing through his young voice.

"You already are someone special, Derek. You won my heart, and I've given it to you for life," she said, kissing his neck as the full moon washed its light over their naked bodies.

"You make me feel special — make me feel as if there's nothing I can't do."

"That's because you're Superman," she told him with a giggle. "Definitely more powerful than a locomotive…"

He laughed, then grew serious again. "What do you say? I'll take care of you if you come with me. We can get married and start our lives in the city," he promised. "You can even go to cooking school and open that café you've always talked about." He grew more excited as he spoke.

Jasmine paused as she thought about what he was asking of her. Could she leave it all behind? If Derek left, though, what would she have to stay for? Nothing worth keeping. She loved her father, but he was so cold most of the time — how much would he miss her, really? He'd eventually get over his anger and their relationship would heal, though it might take a few years.

Derek would have to come back. His father and cousins were here, and they were all closer than most families. The three boys were more siblings than cousins. She'd just be starting a new adventure with the boy she loved, but she wouldn't be cutting her ties here completely.

"Yes. I'll come with you. You have to give me a few days, though," she asked.

Derek pulled her on top of him with a laugh. Jasmine was a little sore, but the pleasure far outweighed the discomfort. The two of them made love beneath the stars, their joy shining even brighter.

They were going to forge a new path for just the two of them. Nothing could keep them from their destiny.

CHAPTER ONE

Ten Years Later

ANOTHER NIGHT, ANOTHER party, though for once probably not another woman. Derek Titan looked around the crowded room and forced himself not to yawn. He couldn't stand attending events where everyone drank too much, laughed too loud and tried far too hard to impress one another.

Derek knew he was what women considered a real catch. Hell, an idiotic magazine had published a write-up on Seattle's most eligible bachelors and ranked him, with his picture, as number one. He'd been furious and had tried to have himself taken out of the article, but his attorney had spouted some crap about freedom of speech. OK, so there were good points in the First Amendment, but he hadn't seen many. Since the article appeared, even more women with their eyes on a prize had approached him.

The magazine listed his net worth as equal to Bill Gates'. Though slightly exaggerated, that part at least was related to business. But of what possible interest or relevance was the hackneyed phrase "tall, dark and handsome"? So what if he stood over six feet and had broad shoulders? He gagged when he read of "rippling muscles." The flipping author even gave advice on how to meet him: don't bother with stalking him at the gym — he hated those places — but take up running, because he ran every morning, and sometimes in the evenings too, as a way to relieve stress.

Though it hinted, at least the article didn't quite say what happened after his second-best way to relieve stress. But here it was — the minute he'd finished taking a woman to bed, he just walked away, and that wasn't something to inspire the magazine's female readership. Sure, a lot of his women tried to get him to stay, but no one held his interest longer than it took him to zip up his pants.

He'd let a woman beat him once at the mating game. And after Jasmine shattered his heart and destroyed his father's business venture, he'd lost interest in the female sex — except, of course, for the sex. His priority had long been revenge. He figured that once he got it, he'd think about settling down.

A woman breezed by him wearing entirely too much perfume, and he snapped back to reality. He sighed, then grabbed a glass of wine from a passing waiter.

These parties were all about who had the most to offer. The women were on the prowl, and the men were fishing. He just wasn't interested.

He watched as a couple of superficial wannabe socialites passed by in low-cut gowns, dripping with diamonds. They were trying to catch his eye, and normally he'd make their day by flirting a little, giving them the impression they stood a chance. Today wasn't that day. He had a raging headache, and he was pissed that he'd been summoned to this snooze-fest.

"There you are, boy. What are you doing hiding in the corner?" Daniel Titan, his father, had walked up to give him the third degree.

"I'm wondering why I'm here when I'd rather be home with a scotch and my feet up," Derek replied.

"You're here because you received a request from your father. I have some things to discuss with you later," Daniel said in his no-nonsense voice.

"And it couldn't wait?" Derek questioned.

"Oh, live a little. You're always so busy adding megabucks to your bank account that you don't stop to smell the cabernet sauvignon," his father said.

"I live it up plenty. Hell, I was in Milan last week."

"You were in Milan on business. That doesn't count," his dad told him.

"For me, the ideal time is mixing business with pleasure," Derek said with a waggle of his eyebrows. Both men relaxed. "Seriously, Dad, I do have a headache. What's so important it couldn't wait until tomorrow morning?"

Once Derek had made his first million, he'd moved his father to the city. Daniel, now the chief financial officer of his huge corporation, had been instrumental in the company's swift and exponential growth. But his dad had gone through hard times more than once while Derek was growing up.

"David Freeman's here tonight, and he's talking to some people, trying to get new investors," Daniel said, his eyes narrowing slightly as he looked at the man who'd destroyed his livelihood some years before.

Derek was on instant alert. He searched the room, spotting his enemy. David was the one who'd made Derek the cutthroat businessman he was. "It's far too late for him. By tomorrow morning, he'll know that his company is mine, no matter what he tries tonight," Derek said.

Derek saw a beautiful woman approach David, stepping up on her tiptoes to kiss him on the cheek. David didn't even bother to turn and acknowledge her. The man noticed nothing around him if it didn't have dollar signs on it, not even his stunning daughter.

Derek's eyes narrowed to slits. He hadn't seen Jasmine for ten years, and those years had been very good to her. It wasn't at all what he'd been expecting, although, with her supreme shallowness, he should have known she'd have focused first and foremost on her appearance.

The top of her dress hugged her body, dipping low in both the front and back. Her curves were even more pronounced now that her body had matured. Her gleaming dark hair was swept up in a classic bun, with tendrils floating around her delicate face. Her chocolate eyes had once mesmerized him. They had a hypnotic quality, with a deceptive innocence shining through the thick lashes.

His gut tightened at just the sight of her, and that outraged him. Was he still a complete fool about her? She'd nearly destroyed his entire family, and yet he still wanted her. But that was all right. After all, his full revenge included her; he would have her in his bed again, and then she'd be begging him not to leave. Shrinks might call it closure. To him, everything was far more primitive.

"I'm leaving now, Dad. There's nothing he can do tonight, and tomorrow's a busy day for me," Derek said. After clasping his father's hand, he turned away and walked from the room without once looking back.

CHAPTER TWO

JASMINE SPOTTED DEREK across the room, and fire and ice waged war within her. How dare he walk around as if he owned the place? She knew the kinder, gentler side of him, but that boy was long gone. He probably never really existed beyond her girlish imagination.

The man she'd spotted tonight wasn't the boy who had taken her virginity and promised her forever. She wished she could forget that summer so many years ago when she'd waited at the abandoned church all day, waited and waited, hoping something had happened to make him late. As the sun had faded from the sky, she'd finally had to admit he wasn't coming. It had all been lies.

Just as her father had said, Derek had told her all he needed to get her to have sex with him. Once he'd added her to his list of conquests, he'd been finished with her. The remembered pain was almost too much to bear, even ten years later.

She watched him turning and walking from the room. He was by far the sexiest man at the party, with his custom tuxedo and piercing blue eyes. Although he sat in an office all day, his body betrayed no hint of softness. Her heart fluttered as she dwelled again on those long summer nights of touching and tasting those hard muscles.

Derek disappeared around the corner just as he'd disappeared that summer ten years before. Back then, she'd believed in fairy tales and magic.

No more.

Jasmine had grown up very wealthy in a small town outside of Seattle, Washington. Her father owned a multimillion-dollar medical-equipment company, and she'd always had more than most people could ever hope for.

Her mother had died while giving birth to her, and her father never remarried. He dated a lot of women, but none of them really acknowledged her existence, so she didn't grow attached to any of them. Sometimes, Jasmine had thought it would be nice to have a woman help her pick out a dress or teach her how to do her hair. But the staff, at least, always spoiled her a bit, which she knew irritated her father.

She'd seen Derek in school from the time she was young, but she got to know him only the summer before her senior year in high school. His family was dirt poor, but he was always determined to make a success out of his life and turn things around. He ended up helping her with math, and soon they were fast friends. She'd loved his hunger and motivation and the way he never talked down about anyone. She thought he was every one of her fairy-tale heroes come to life.

Soon, she found she was spending every waking moment with him. When her father found out she was dating a boy from the poor side of town, he'd been furious and demanded that she end the relationship. It was the first time in her life her father told her she couldn't have something she wanted. It also was the first time she'd defied him.

She'd continued to see Derek behind her father's back. She loved that Derek seemed to like her for who she was and not for her money. He wouldn't let her spend money on him — ever. He worked hard for a construction company, which would frustrate her at times because she wanted him to be with her and not at a job. He'd laugh at her frustration, but he always made it up to her on the weekends.

"Jasmine?"

Jasmine turned to find that she'd completely tuned out of the conversation. Normally, she was the epitome of cool — making sure to schmooze with her father's investors. That was her job at these functions.

More than once she'd had to fend off the advances of some dirty old man. It was a source of contention between her father and her — just one of many.

She wouldn't sell her soul to the devil, even if the devil was dressed in a hand-tailored business suit. Money had its uses, and she certainly needed a lot more than she had, but she wasn't for sale, not at any price.

"I'm sorry. I have a slight headache tonight and it's made me lose focus," she answered sweetly to the sixty-year-old who was leering at her. She had to fight the shiver threatening to travel down her spine at the lust in his eyes.

"I was just telling your father that I would love to have the two of you up to my lake house sometime real soon."

No way in hell! That is what she wanted to say.

"That sounds like a very pleasant weekend. Make sure you have my father notify me of when," she answered instead, already planning a convenient illness.

The man beamed at her; his hand came up to rest on her upper arm, and then his finger trailed downward.

"Excuse me. I need some medicine for this annoying headache," she said, discreetly extracting herself from the man's slimy grip and walking away. She was on the verge of being sick. How many more of these functions would she have to attend before she'd had enough?

Seeing Derek tonight had been too much. Wasn't time supposed to heal all wounds? In her case, ten years obviously hadn't been enough time. Seeing her first love — the only man she'd ever loved — was just too much.

It was time to leave.

Tomorrow would be a better day. That had become her motto for the last decade. One of these days, maybe it would.

As she walked from the party, Jasmine thought back to the day that her innocence had been stolen from her, the day that she'd realized she couldn't trust her heart, and she certainly couldn't trust men…

CHAPTER THREE

ARRIVING HOME AFTER being out all night, Jasmine felt her knees shaking. As she stepped through the doorway, her father was standing there, his face blotched with color, and spittle flying from his lips.

"I love him, Dad," she said, firming her shoulders as she faced down the man who instilled the very meaning of the word *fear* inside her.

"You don't know what love is. You are only seventeen," he shouted, stepping closer.

For the first time, she feared he might strike her. He'd never been a caring or engaged parent, but he'd never physically abused her.

"We're going to get married." She knew she couldn't just run away now. If she wanted to be a grown-up, then she needed to make grown-up decisions.

For a moment, his face got even redder, and then his shoulders sagged as he looked at her, anger seeming to fade away as sorrow filled his features.

"Have I been that terrible a father?"

"No, it isn't that, Dad. It's just that Derek and I want to be together. His father is starting a new business, so Derek can leave feeling right about it, and he's going to the city to make something of himself. He will do it, too. He's smart and strong and brings me such joy," she said. Maybe her father would really listen to her for once.

Walking over to her, he leaned down and kissed her cheek. "When did you grow up?" he whispered, making her heart leap.

She had never thought he'd be so willing to accept her decision. She'd thought that she would be leaving the house with him hating her, that it would take years for them to reconcile. She loved Derek enough to risk that, but the thought still saddened her.

"I don't know. Being with Derek is just…just like bees and honey. We fit and he makes me feel grown." What better explanation was there?

"What is this business his father is attempting? Maybe I can help in some way."

In her excitement to earn her father's approval, she never once thought he could be up to no good. This was her dad — the man who had raised her.

"I'm not sure exactly. It's a computer store, I think."

"I will speak to the bank, make sure the loan goes through for his new business."

"You'll do that, Dad?" How could she ever have thought her father cold or uncaring?

"There isn't anything I won't do to make you happy, princess," he assured her.

They spoke long into the night. She told her father everything, how she and Derek would meet at the church — all of it. Her dad kissed her goodnight and she fell asleep while still planning the future.

That night she called Derek and told him she had a surprise for him, that he would find out at the church when they met. He tried to get her to talk about it, but her dad had told her it would be more meaningful if she did it in person on the day they started their new life.

Because she now had her dad's permission, she thought it a little silly to meet at the church instead of just having him pick her up, but in her romantic heart, it was what she wanted to do, and her father agreed. The church signified the start of a new life.

She anticipated the surprise on Derek's face, and the joy that would flow through him.

Two days later, Jasmine had her bags packed and went in to tell her father goodbye. He hadn't always been the best father, but he had still raised her all on his own, and her eyes filled with tears as she approached him.

"It's time, Dad," she whispered, amazed by how much it hurt to leave. The ecstasy of being with Derek forever outweighed the pain, though. And now there wouldn't be any estrangement; her father was supporting her all the way.

"I can't believe you are moving to the city. Just remember your promise. You won't get married without me there." David was all smiles as he spoke to his daughter.

"I am so happy you want to be there," she said, throwing her arms around his neck.

"I couldn't miss my baby girl's wedding. Before you go meet Derek, can you do me a favor first? I have an important package that needs to be signed for and I have to run to City Hall for a meeting. Would you wait for it before you go?"

Derek didn't have a cell phone, and she couldn't reach him at his house, but he would be fine if she ran a little late. He knew from experience that she wasn't always punctual, and he'd understand. This was a last request from her dad, and they were parting on good terms.

"Of course, Dad. When will the package arrive?"

"It shouldn't be more than an hour," he promised before kissing her cheek again and then heading out the door.

It was two hours. Jasmine rushed out the door, and made her way to the church fueled by excitement. She carried only a backpack and a small suitcase filled with items she'd need the most. Her father said he'd send the rest when they reached their destination. Fueled by young love and needing nothing more, she was off.

She couldn't believe how good her father was being about all of this.

Derek wasn't there when she arrived, but Jasmine wasn't worried. He'd probably gotten held up, just as she had. Sitting down on the broken church steps, she looked out at the surrounding woods, listening to the sounds of birds chirping, and squirrels scampering through the tree branches.

When an hour passed, she began to grow concerned. Derek was always on time, and this was a big day for the two of them. Wouldn't he send one of his cousins if he were going to be this late? She couldn't imagine that he'd have come and gone. He would have waited, knowing she had been held up since that had often happened while they were dating.

When the sun started to set, she didn't even notice the tears tracking down her face. Maybe he'd changed his mind. Why? What could have possibly made him do such a thing?

She finally accepted he wasn't coming and dragged herself home, crying the entire way. When she walked into the house and her father saw her, he took her into his arms, cradling her the way he'd done when she was a small child.

"What's wrong, Jasmine?" His voice was full of concern.

"He wasn't there. I don't understand," she said between sobs.

"Oh, sweetie, this is what I was worried about," he cooed, making her cry all that much harder.

When she couldn't cry anymore, she made her way to her room and lay alone on her bed, clutching the one picture she had of Derek and her to her heart. Something had to be wrong. He wouldn't have left her there without a valid reason.

Working up the courage to call, she sat with the phone in her hand for almost an hour. Finally, she dialed his house and sat there, holding her breath, as it rang on the other end.

"Hello?" It was Derek. He was home!

She began to smile. Something had come up. It wasn't that he'd left without her.

"Derek?" she barely whispered. Her throat was raw from all the tears she'd shed.

"I have nothing to say to you," he growled into the phone.

"I…I don't understand," she choked out. Never before had she heard him sound so cruel. His voice was nearly devoid of emotion, just an icy chill running through the line of the telephone.

"You and your father are scum. You'll one day reap what you sow."

The call disconnected and Jasmine stared at the phone for what must have been forever.

"Jasmine?" She looked up to find her dad in the doorway.

"I…What… He sounded so horrible," she said, looking at her dad for answers.

"You shouldn't have called. He made his decision when he left you waiting for him. I never trusted the boy. That's why I had wanted to keep you apart, and I shouldn't have relented, shouldn't have hoped that he was different. Boys like him want one thing, and once they get it, they throw the girls away like they are nothing more than trash. You are better off without him, Jasmine. You'll come to see that soon. We'll just move forward now."

Jasmine lay back down as her father shut the door. Maybe he was right. Maybe Derek had gotten all he'd wanted and he was now done. Sobbing until exhaustion pulled her under, Jasmine felt she'd lost her innocence that night. Her days of being a trusting teenage girl were gone forever.

The Tycoon's Revenge paperback is now available.
The eBook is availabe for free at all major online retailers.

46022736R00145

Made in the USA
Lexington, KY
20 October 2015